A Dark Angel

Ted Lovett did not know, of course, that last morning when he awoke that he would be dead and buried by midnight. Who knows such things? Who knows anything, really, about what it means to die? Ted, although a smart guy and far from superficial, had not thought much about death. He wasn't that old—nineteen—and his interests dealt mainly with the *real* world: sun and fun; girls and school; the living and the breathing. Still, like everyone else on the planet—only decades premature—he would end up in a dark box in the damp ground, not moving, not knowing, a forgotten form—kept alive only in painful memories. Sadly, but perhaps fittingly, the love of his life would put him in his grave.

Books by Christopher Pike

BURY ME DEEP
CHAIN LETTER 2: THE ANCIENT EVIL
DIE SOFTLY
THE ETERNAL ENEMY
EXECUTION OF INNOCENCE
FALL INTO DARKNESS
FINAL FRIENDS #1: THE PARTY
FINAL FRIENDS #2: THE DANCE
FINAL FRIENDS #3: THE GRADUATION
GIMME A KISS
THE GRAVE
THE HOLLOW SKULL
THE IMMORTAL
LAST ACT
THE LAST VAMPIRE
THE LAST VAMPIRE 2: BLACK BLOOD
THE LAST VAMPIRE 3: RED DICE
THE LAST VAMPIRE 4: PHANTOM
THE LAST VAMPIRE 5: EVIL THIRST
THE LAST VAMPIRE 6: CREATURES OF FOREVER
THE LOST MIND
MAGIC FIRE
MASTER OF MURDER
THE MIDNIGHT CLUB
MONSTER
REMEMBER ME
REMEMBER ME 2: THE RETURN
REMEMBER ME 3: THE LAST STORY
ROAD TO NOWHERE
SCAVENGER HUNT
SEE YOU LATER
SPELLBOUND
THE STAR GROUP
THE STARLIGHT CRYSTAL
THE TACHYON WEB
TALES OF TERROR #1
TALES OF TERROR #2
THE VISITOR
WHISPER OF DEATH
THE WICKED HEART
WITCH

Available from ARCHWAY Paperbacks

Christopher Pike

The Grave

AN ARCHWAY PAPERBACK
Published by POCKET BOOKS
New York London Toronto Sydney Tokyo Singapore

AN ARCHWAY PAPERBACK *Original*

An Archway Paperback published by
POCKET BOOKS, a division of Simon & Schuster Inc.
1230 Avenue of the Americas, New York, NY 10020

Copyright © 1999 by Christopher Pike

All rights reserved, including the right to reproduce
this book or portions thereof in any form whatsoever.
For information address Pocket Books, 1230 Avenue
of the Americas, New York, NY 10020

ISBN: 0-671-55077-2

First Archway Paperback printing September 1999

10 9 8 7 6 5 4 3

AN ARCHWAY PAPERBACK and colophon are
registered trademarks of Simon & Schuster Inc.

Cover art by Franco Accornero

Printed in the U.S.A.

IL 14+

For Brendan,
who always made me laugh.

The Grave

1

Ted Lovett did not know, of course, that last morning when he awoke that he would be dead and buried by midnight. Who knows such things? Who knows anything, really, about what it means to die? Ted, although a smart guy and far from superficial, had not thought much about death. He wasn't that old—nineteen—and his interests dealt mainly with the *real* world: sun and fun; girls and school; the living and the breathing. Still, like everyone else on the planet—only decades premature—he would end up in a dark box in the damp ground, not moving, not knowing, a forgotten form—kept alive only in painful memories. Sadly, but perhaps fittingly, the love of his life would put him in his grave.

Her name was Dara Smith, so she said, but she lied about so much else she might have lied about that. Because he had known her only a month, before he died, she could not really be called his true love, but he thought of her that way nevertheless. Working his way through his first year of college as an electrician's apprentice, he met her at a job site, a half-built house near the ocean in Santa Monica. She just happened by, while he was retrieving a spool of wire from his boss's truck, and asked the time. An innocent entry into tragedy—so much the better, maybe, for her.

Darling Dara—her hair long and permed, tossed by the ocean breeze, the color of simmering corn on the cob, invisible steam rising through blond curls. But she was no California cliché hiking up from the beach that day. On the pale side, she had lips that though wide and generous, were too straight, hiding emotions kept in line only by a strong will. Her green eyes sparkled, but only on cue. She had a detached air about her, something Ted noticed in two seconds. But cool is not cold, and he thought she smiled at him when she asked the time. He set down his spool of wire and wiped his hands on his blue work pants. He did not have a watch, no matter, he could guess.

"I think it's about two-twenty," he said. "We just had lunch."

"OK." She did not immediately move on, for which he was glad. Instead, she clasped her hands together and let them hang as she *seemed* to study him. Her clothes were odd, an expensive maroon blouse fell over baggy white pants with holes. She was skinny—her top hung loose over her chest, nothing to complain about there, though. What-ever—she was incredibly pretty and appeared in no hurry to get away from him. She added, "What did you have for lunch?"

"A Subway sandwich. There's one around the corner. The contractor on this job picks them up for us free." He paused. "I had roast beef today."

"I'm a vegetarian."

"Really? That's cool. A lot of people are these days. I'm trying to eat less meat myself, more fish."

"That's not meat?" she asked.

He stuttered. "I-I don't think so. Well, maybe it is, to the fish at least." He forced a laugh. "I don't think about food that much, to tell you the truth, except when I'm hungry."

She moved a step closer unexpectedly—it brought her pretty close indeed. He immediately noticed her breath, the smell of which was always to remind him of Dara—peppermint candy kisses, all the promise just the smile of a pretty girl could bring to a lonely boy. He actually felt her breath on his cheek and wondered if she was interested in him. The thought, or something else, made him shiver.

"Are you hungry now?" she asked.

"No." He took a breath. "I told you, I just ate."

"Oh." She withdrew slightly and seemed sad. She stared at the sunlit ocean between the houses, glit-tering sunbeams on dreamy blue. She added, "I haven't eaten."

Ted thought that he could eat again, if she

wanted him to. He asked, "Do you live around here?"

Her eyes were not on him. "No."

"I do, only a couple of miles from here." He added, "What brings you to this part of town?"

"Friends."

"They live around here?"

She nodded and came back to him. "They hang out here."

"It's a great neighborhood," he said gamely. "Where do you live?"

"Not far away." She offered her hand. "I'm Dara Smith."

They shook briefly. "Ted Lovett. Nice to meet you."

"Nice to meet you, Ted."

Pleasant, the way she said his name, like it meant something to her.

"I wish I had a watch and could give you the exact time," he said, desperate for something intelligent to say. He hadn't dated much and was clumsy around girls. But Dara did not seem to mind, although her gaze did stray back to the water. It seemed to hold a special fascination for her. A halo of melancholy clung to her—a wounded angel, he thought, hopefully one who needed his help.

That was another thing that struck him about Dara from the beginning. Her coolness did not affect her vulnerability. She appeared strong but lost—without contradiction. He feared to lose her, to have her walk away. He did not believe in love at first sight, but something was going on here. He was not overly emotional, but he already liked her a lot, more than logic or lust could explain. How to ask her out? She might say no, and then—then he would feel like shit.

"It doesn't matter," she said after a long pause. She could have been referring to something other than the time, life itself maybe, that all life was hopeless. Her voice was soft and smooth; it touched him without human feeling. Still, it touched him deeply.

"I'd like to talk to you some more," Ted said, glancing over his shoulder in the direction of the house. His boss was not in sight, but he knew how impatient the man could be. Ted picked up the wire again and tried to look like an important job was desperately waiting for him. He was not so much trying to get away from Dara as he was hoping to show her he was somebody. Really, the thought of her rejecting him was too much for him.

She put a hand on his arm and stared up at him. "Can I see you again?" she asked.

He should have died right then. He could have, but the gods were not kind. In fact, if the world was any example, the gods were crazy. Love is seldom kind, he was to think later, when he was dying, choking on horror and slowly suffocating three feet under. Love killed more than it saved—it was a curse. When she touched him, although he did not know it, her curse entered into him and changed him forever. Yet all he felt in that moment was joy. This wonderful girl liked him. What a wonderful life it was. His face flushed with blood—had she been a vampire she could have licked his brow for lunch.

"Sure," he said. "I'd like that. Would you like to see a movie or something?"

A small smile, sad at the edges. "Yes, that would be nice. Can I call you?"

"Yeah. Or I can call you, if that would be OK?"

She stared past him, "I'll call you. Tonight."

"OK." He gave her his number, and she said she would remember it. He sure hoped so. As he watched her walk away, he tried to understand the pain he felt in his chest. He was still happy but it was as if a portion of her sorrow now grew inside him. He didn't mind, though, he wanted to share many things with her, the good and the bad, in sickness and in health, all that—he would drive her to Las Vegas and marry her if she asked, finish school later. He hoped she would give him the chance to get to know her. He hoped a lot of things, that made no difference in the end.

Not to the grave that waited for Ted.

She did call, and he went out with her the following night, to an Italian restaurant not far from the beach and his parents' house. He met her at the restaurant—she insisted on it. He wondered if she lived with someone and wanted to keep it from him. While talking, she seldom volunteered information, yet his life appeared to interest her. She listened with wide green eyes as he spoke of studying engineering at UCLA, his classes and teachers. It was as if she were proud of him, but regretful that she had nothing to share. He did learn, however, that she was an artist who worked for a special-effects house in the valley. Her working made him ask about her age. The question did not seem to bother her, although she did not answer it.

"How old do you think I am?" she asked. They ate outside, the evening warm and still, light pedestrian traffic on the nearby sidewalk, a candle flickering in a votive holder between them. She wore black but was casually dressed. His shirt was new and stiff, his mother had bought it for him, wished him well on his big date. Ted really loved his parents, and of course, they loved their only child.

"My mother once warned me never to guess a woman's age."

"But I give you permission."

"Well," he said. "Twenty?"

"No."

"Older?"

"Guess," she said.

"Younger?"

"Ah. Enough guesses. I won't tell you."

"Why not?"

Her eyes slipped away, far away. "It doesn't matter."

What did matter to Darling Dara? Half the evening he wondered if he should try to kiss her when they parted, but she made the first move. Not a brief or shallow kiss, no—she got inside him and was a nonvegetarian meal roasting over a crackling fire. Plus those sweet peppermints—who would have guessed that she would later toss one in his coffin for remembrance? Cruelty in beauty, nature's great tease—the rose that pricks, the thorn that ca-resses, simple lies that worked well on the young and foolish. Yeah, she had his number and then some, what a sucker he was. But he felt so alive when he kissed her; it was supernatural to feel him-self being sucked into her and not care that he might not come up for air. Her heart, as she pressed her chest to his for a final embrace, beat against his ribs in gentle agony. Her mouth was wet and warm, he believed in her passion. She was not a vampire or an angel, he thought, she was alive. And she was his, at least for that moment when he held her.

They said goodbye on the street beside his car.

She said she would call soon.

Could he call her? Soon, Ted, she answered.

The darkness swallowed her up as she walked away.

He thought about following. Smart idea.

But he wanted to trust her. Love her.

"Good night, Dara," he whispered to her back.

She would wish him the same, as *they* put him in the box.

Three weeks before he died, and he had no idea.

Pain—waiting for her to call. He loved it and he hated it. He felt so many emotions he was worn out. He would fall asleep each night dreaming of her lying beside him. But he didn't know where she lived or worked. She waited five days before she called again; five long years to him. He was angry and frustrated, but he didn't let it show in his voice, because he was overjoyed as well. She wanted to see him that night. She wanted him, he thought. She asked to meet him at the same restaurant. What the hell, he thought, the food was good.

They went to a movie after dinner and walked on the beach after the show. What was there to talk about? He wanted to talk, to understand her better, but Dara was off in silence, or else silence had found them both. It was as if her aura lived in solitude even when she was with someone in the midst of the city. The beach was empty as they strolled along the water's edge. For the tenth time he tried to strike up a meaningful conversation, but she hardly responded. Yes . . . no . . . it doesn't matter.

When the half-moon rose, however, and hovered over a nearby hill, she paused and clasped his hand. Yet she did not speak, not for a long time, and then when she did he didn't understand what she meant.

"The moon is a mirror," she said.

"What?"

"It only shines because of the sun." She held his hand tighter and added, "The moon is a liar."

"Why do you say that?"

"It's always changing. Sometimes it is big and bright, sometimes you can hardly see it." She gestured. "I hate it."

He forced a smile. He forced a lot with Dara, but he felt he had to. "Hate is a strong word to apply to the moon, don't you think?"

"No." She let go of his hand but leaned over and kissed his cheek. Tonight her lips were cold. "I hate life as well. It's a lie."

He worried that she was depressed, but her tone was not simply one of a person depressed. In fact, he really could not figure out her mood at all. Classifying Dara was like trying to classify the various shades of moonlight. In so many ways she seemed a creature of the night.

"But you must love some things," he protested.

"No." She ran a hand through his hair. "I can't feel love anymore."

He chuckled uneasily. "I don't believe that."

"Believe it, Ted. I'm not like any girl you know."

"I can believe that. But you're not cold. I wouldn't be attracted to you if you were." He had confessed a portion of his feelings without intending to. Hell, it was done. He added hastily, "You must love your art. You wouldn't do it if you didn't love it."

"I haven't drawn in a year."

"But your job in the . . ."

"I lied," she interrupted. She rose up on her toes and brought her face near his. "Kiss me; love me."

He kissed her, doing what she wanted without being asked. But she drew away too soon and stepped back to the edge of the water. Kicking off her shoes, she let the cold foam run over her feet. He remained a step back.

"You should get away from me," she said with her back to him. "I'm not good for you."

That hurt. "You don't know that. Neither of us does."

"You're wrong. I know." She paused. "If you stay with me, you'll die."

He forced another laugh, although her words cut him cold. "How will I die?"

She turned and stared, the hateful moon in her eyes. "Horribly."

They kissed some more in his car, and she lowered his head and let him touch her breasts. They were more than he believed he deserved. Still, she was aloof; he wasn't sure if she felt anything even in a moment of passion. Her sighs of pleasure sounded distant. But he felt he could not withdraw, only go that distance, to the edge of the abyss, to reach her. He did not for a moment believe she would hurt him.

Their third date was two weeks later. The call came out of the blue, when he was sure he would never hear from her again. She asked if they could meet at the restaurant once more. *No* shouted in his brain; *yes* came out of his mouth. She wanted to see him in an hour. On the way out of the house, his mother stopped him. She'd had him when she was forty-three and his dad was fifty. At his high school graduation people had thought they were his grandparents. His mother looked even older than her sixty-two years—she had always worried too much, about everything, especially him. She wanted to know when they could meet this mystery girl.

"Maybe next time." Ted shrugged. "She's kind of shy."

His mother studied him. "She has you all wrapped up inside. You know that."

He lowered his head. "She's not like anyone I've ever met."

11

His mother hesitated, then hugged him. "Just take care of yourself, Ted."

He smiled at her concern. "She's not that strange."

His mother didn't look convinced. "You haven't been yourself since you started dating her."

He didn't argue. He hadn't felt normal. His dreams, especially, had changed since he met Dara. There was no color in them, only black and white sharp edges, harsh voices, and tense nerves, as if his nocturnal senses had been amplified while simultaneously drained. He didn't understand why he kept dreaming of a dark man standing in a light-filled doorway, a silhouette cut from perverse paper. In his nightmare—for he always woke from it sweating—he felt he knew this dark man better than anyone in the world because he had helped create him. Yet he didn't know the man's name, and in the dream his own name was different. He was . . . he could not remember.

Possibly because it didn't matter. Not then.

He kissed his mother goodbye. He never saw her again.

They met at the restaurant but did not eat. It was late, already past nine, and Dara wanted to go for a drive. Where, he wondered. She would show him. He had grown up close to the Santa Monica Mountains, but she directed him along a narrow road he had never seen before. Half an hour after meeting her they were far from the city. When the road dead-ended in a cluster of trees, they got out. There was no moon, but the stars shone with unusual clarity. Ted felt the air was electrically charged; it did not appear to radiate from Dara alone. Halloween had come two weeks early, and not all monsters wore costumes. It was as if the trees themselves were in foul moods. He wished he knew where he and Dara were going as he stumbled along in the dark, his hand in Dara's. They had not brought a flashlight, although he told her they should. He had one in his car trunk, but she shook her head no. Now he felt they would get lost.

Yet her hand was good to hold.

"Where are we going?" he asked halfway up the side of a steep hill. He was in good shape, but the going was rough and he panted. Dara remained cool and calm, however, and he assumed she knew the terrain well. He wondered if she was taking him to an isolated spot to seduce him—it was a pleasant thought. She peered at him in the dark and patted him on the shoulder with her free hand.

"It's not far," she said.

"What is it?"

She hesitated. "A burial ground."

"Is it Indian?"

"No."

"What is it then? Why are we going there?"

She squeezed his hand. "You'll see when we get there."

They hiked for another forty minutes, and by then he was tired and thirsty. It was another warm autumn night; the dry brush crackled loudly beneath their feet. They were not following a path, and he didn't understand how Dara could know which way they were going. But she did seem to be able to see much better in the dark than he.

Suddenly they stopped in a circular clearing. The branches of the trees hung low, just above their heads—he could see their shadows against the black of the sky. The air was incredibly still, painfully so—his heart pounded and his breath sawed ragged. Still, he was happy to be alone with Dara. Always, no matter how uncomfortable she made him feel, he still cared for her. She let go of his hand and moved closer, and he felt her lips on the side of his face.

"I wish you did not have to be afraid," she whispered.

He took a breath. "Of what? You?"

"No. Of death."

He smiled in the dark. "Death doesn't scare me."

"It will." She kissed him softly. "It will."

He heard a noise off to his right, disturbed leaves; footsteps were at his back; a giggle on his left. All the sounds came to him at once; he didn't know which way to turn. For he could see nothing, only the outline of Dara. But he sensed one thing immediately—he was surrounded, and those who were coming were coming for him. Dara had led him to them. She had given him enough hints.

Strong hands grabbed him from behind and yanked his arms back. He tried to resist, but a thick fist plunged deep into his solar plexus and breathless agony shot through his guts. He would have doubled over and fallen to the ground writhing had he been allowed, but those at his back were pulling his arms back and out of their sockets. His vision colored red, the stars overhead turned to daggers, and the surrounding trees spun as if he were on a defective carousel. The need to breathe, to get air in his lungs, screamed in his brain. He had never been so scared in his life.

"Rip off his clothes!" a young man ordered from his side.

The command came just as Ted managed to draw in a feeble amount of air. He felt more than heard a large rip between his shoulder blades. Hands clawed at his pants—someone stuck a knife in his waistband near his groin and began to cut the material. Tearing was followed by atrocity—his pants and underwear were pulled down while his shirt was ripped from his body. His sweat-soaked skin stung in the night air. There seemed to be thousands of hands on him, although he could see no one clearly, only a mass of dark heads, groping limbs. He did not know where Dara was.

In seconds he was stripped naked. They even pulled off his shoes. He made the mistake of trying to kick his assailants and received another crushing blow to the stomach. This time he vomited, all over himself, while the invisible gang jeered. He could not have imagined such pain.

"Smear him with the pig's blood!" a guy shouted.

Oh God, Ted thought, gasping for breath. This could not be happening to him! He had done nothing wrong! What did these people want with him? Of course he knew the answer to that, they were going to torture him, sacrifice him, kill him. Pig's blood—they must be Satanists. From multiple directions, he felt himself being slapped with warm sticky blood. It seemed to slip in through his pores and poison his soul. Some of the blood was his own. He took a hard blow to the face—his shattered nose dripped freely. He felt his stomach rise again with bile. But all that came out was a cry of anguish.

"Please don't," he wept.

They laughed; they liked it that he was terrified. Their cruelty was unreal, for none of them sounded that old. They were teenagers like himself, probably some were still in high school. Yet they were ageless, devils who had centuries ago crawled up from a stinking pit in hell. The way they tossed him around—it was as if they each had the strength of five people. He kept telling himself that he would wake up any second and be home in bed. Under the blankets, where he had imagined for the last weeks that he was alone with Dara. His Darling Demon, why didn't she come to his rescue?

An entire bucket of blood was poured over his head and he choked on it. The blood was fresh— even as he inhaled it a part of him realized that the animal had not been killed long ago.

"Put him in the coffin!" the same guy yelled. "Put him in the ground!"

What was left of Ted cracked then. They were going to bury him alive! Once more he struggled to break free, but he was made of straw and they were steel. His legs were lifted in the air and his midsection was thrust toward the sky. He felt a sharp stab in his lower back, a knife, perhaps searching to cut his spinal cord. The stars, seen through the film of blood, glared down at him like grotesque holes poked through a canopy of reality. They carried him partway across the narrow meadow and then he was thrown down into a narrow wooden box. How vain were his struggles—they held him in place with two hands. So the coffin had been waiting for him all along, and Dara had known exactly what had been planned for him. How he hated her right then. Yet it was to her he made his final plea for life.

"Dara!" he screamed.

The insane crowd quieted. A torch was struck and the flame illumined a portion of the sick cult. He saw perhaps ten of them—all naked, smeared with the same blood as he was, their grins wide with hysteria. He glimpsed a young man with curly blond hair that reminded him of Dara's hair—then her face swam into view. Kneeling beside his coffin—he understood now that it was his, that it was all that was his—she leaned over and wiped blood from his eyes,. She alone was still dressed, wearing the same blue dress she'd had on when they met at the restaurant earlier. A profound sorrow lay on her face as he strove in vain to find compassion there. Obviously her pain over the night's events could not be directly translated into human feelings. Only then did he realize she might not be human.

"I told you to stay away from me," she said.

"But why?" he wept.

She shook her head slightly.

"Good night, Ted," she said softly.

She leaned over and kissed his forehead.

Then dropped a peppermint in his coffin.

Dara stood and disappeared in the crowd. The young man with blond curls and green eyes snapped at the others to continue the ritual. Ted saw a long board pass overhead, and it was the last thing he saw before the torch and the world was cut off. Naturally, he was no longer held down but the coffin lid went on quickly. The depth of the box was shallow—he could get no leverage with his legs or arms, to push against it. What did it matter anyway? *They* were holding it in place; *they* were nailing the lid shut. He was in a place of utter blackness.

He heard the nails splinter into the wood beside his head and began to scream and could not stop. They had more than one hammer, a bag full of nails. The lid was fastened in place in less than a minute. He was lifted up once more, the coffin carried a few feet, then he felt himself being slowly lowered into a shallow grave. It was only when they tossed dirt on the top of the coffin that he heard the chant.

The tone was guttural and thick, monotonous yet hypnotic—so primeval it could have originated before mankind, from aliens, the last rites of a race of intelligent serpents. They were praying, he realized, that he would die and go to hell. That he would in turn become like them, and one day awake from death, a rotten corpse with every last morsel of flesh eaten from his body by worms, to walk the world at night. A hideous wraith. To hurt people, to lie to people, to kill people. They prayed to Satan while he wished he could pray to God.

But all he could do was scream.

The shovelfuls of dirt rained down.

The chant droned on. Horror tore at his throat.

The air in the coffin could not last.

Matter began to slow. Mind to collapse.

Time narrowed and slipped through a crack.

Soon the grave was covered over.

Ted died. The others departed.

All was silence. Blessed silence.

2

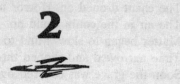

Keri Weir was seventeen, a high school senior, an ex-cheerleader, an employee at a music store, and confused about life. The latter uncertainty centered on three things: her mother was a drug addict; she never had any money, even by teen standards; and she didn't know if she liked her boyfriend, never mind loved him. Oh, of course she liked Clay, he was an extremely nice guy. That was half the problem: he was like a puppy dog, too eager to please. He was so devoted to her that she lived in a constant state of guilt because she didn't feel the same way. But she had to wonder if any sane person could feel the way Clay did. Clay Stanton seldom visited her without freshly picked flowers in hand. She wasn't even that crazy about flowers, and should tell him, she thought.

She probably should tell him that she needed a break.

From him—for five years. God, it would kill him.

Her mother was another issue. When her big-time lawyer dad had run off with his buxom secretary, he left them a sizable chunk of money, but her mom had chosen to invest recklessly in powders for her nose. In other words she had snorted so much cocaine in the last two years that the cartilage in her nose had melted into the rest of her face. A high-priced plastic surgeon had repaired the damage, but since her mother continued to get high it was just a matter of time before she blew a major vessel in her brain. Mom had already sold their house and practically everything in the house to pay for the drugs. Keri slept on a mat on the floor of their crummy apartment—one day she had come home from school to see her bedroom set being carried out to a moving van. Gee whiz, for a moment she had thought they were moving back into a nice house in a classy neighborhood.

Her father didn't want to hear about it. New wife, new kid—what did he need with their problems? That's what he said at least, but a part of Keri liked to think he still cared. But she did agree with him that sending more money was not the answer. That would just kill her mother faster. As it was Keri suspected her mom's new pusher was a part-time pimp, and that her mom was selling her body for cocaine. It was a thought Keri tried not to have too often, and definitely something she hadn't told her father.

21

So she had problems and no solutions. The reason she dropped out of cheerleading had been so she could work full-time, not easy when she was still carrying a full load of honors classes at school. It was still the first quarter and already she was doing poorly—by her almost straight-A standards. The select scholarships at the best schools were not going to come knocking, after all. Not unless something major changed and fast. Yet there was no way to sober her mom up because the woman did not want to get better. Indeed, she'd said on several occasions that she wanted to die. Keri's mother had loved her father very much.

Life was a bitch, and then you were supposed to die. That's what the Bible said, at least in Keri's version, then again she had never been very religious. She hadn't even prayed for Debra, her sister, when she died two years ago. Just didn't think there was anyone there to listen to what she had to say. Debra was dust, God was a hollow ghost, accept it, that was her motto. There were no miracles, nothing ever really changed unless one made it change. That was fair, though, she thought, she had to make her own life happen.

But rearranging the CDs at work that Friday afternoon when she met Oscar, she reflected hard on her life and wondered if it would be any different a year from then. It was a scary thought.

When Oscar came into the store, she thought he was an interesting-looking guy, maybe twenty, with long brown hair and broad shoulders. Yet he was thin, and the first thing she noticed about him—

even from halfway across the store—was how long and bony his hands were. They were exquisite hands nevertheless—she decided he must be an artist of some sort. The lack of fat on his face hollowed his eyes—they were gray and serious. It was as if he were scanning the music store with a specific purpose in mind, other than CDs and videos. When his eyes passed over her, they didn't pause. She didn't care; it wasn't as if he was so handsome that she wanted to spill a rack of movies so that he'd feel obliged to help her pick them up. His clothes hung loose on his lanky frame, a worn brown jacket, tan slacks, a white shirt he must have bought before his overzealous diet. He turned and headed toward the old movies, black-and-white classics. The store was having a sale on them—maybe that was what had brought him in.

Keri was good at talking to people. She had confidence in her intelligence and her looks—in that order. Her face was also thin, and her nose was a shade large for her face, but she had a great smile, a wide mouth, and her long brown hair was fine and shiny. No breasts, though, both her parents were of slight builds. Guys liked her and asked her out, behind Clay's back and sometimes in front of him. She never went, though. Because her mother could die any night guilt was her shadow, and she was determined not to hurt Clay more than she already had. Yet she often wondered if it was already too late for that, if she should have told him six months ago that they could never be more than friends. Of course she should have told him that before she slept with him—twice, three months ago. Boy, that had been a mistake, and not even that much fun. He had cried both times, not from happiness. She had wanted a cigarette and didn't even smoke.

Keri continued to clean up the CD racks. She didn't understand teenagers, hardly related to them even though she was one chronologically. They were such slobs—they plowed through the various artists, carrying on about how great the latest hot singer was, and then couldn't be bothered putting their god's music back in the right place. Keri felt like a mature adult trapped in a cheerleader's body. When she occasionally snapped at her more sloppy customers, they looked at her with surprise. Like she didn't belong in their age group. She supposed the stress of her life was to blame. For sure, she couldn't blame Clay, he would have loved nothing more than to help her with her work, and she had to shoo him away to keep him from showing up to help.

She ended up standing close to the thin guy as he studied his movies. She appraised him from the side, ten feet away, thought once again how pale he was, how utterly cool his high cheekbones were. His gray eyes were not bright, but they did dominate his face with their depth, their slow but deliberate movements. He was not glancing at the titles, he was slowly and methodically drinking them in. His right bony hand reached out for a title and she was surprised but pleased to see he had chosen *To Kill a Mockingbird,* which had always been one of her favorites. The words just burst out of her mouth.

"I love that movie," she said. "Have you seen it?"

He glanced over and nodded slightly. "Yes."

She came a step closer. "You like old movies? I love them best. I think Hollywood lost something when it switched to color. Have you seen *Citizen Kane?* Many people consider it the finest movie ever made. Orson Welles was a genius."

"I have seen it, yes," he said.

His voice unnerved her; she tried to pinpoint why but could not. Obviously he was serious, so few people their age were. Yet his voice was somehow familiar, a sound heard long ago but forgotten.

"What did you think of it?" she asked.

"It was very good."

"What did you think of *To Kill a Mockingbird?*"

"Tragic. Moving."

"Do you like tragedies?"

He lowered his eyes. "I don't seek them out."

Cool answer, she thought. She might have hit a button; he looked like someone who had suffered, which was not to say he appeared depressed, but rather, wise.

"What's your name?" she asked.

He looked up. "Oscar."

She offered her hand. "I'm Keri, I work here." She gestured to her name tag with her free hand. "As if that was a mystery." He had a strong handshake, for such a skinny guy. But he didn't hold on to her hand for very long. She wondered if she was annoying him and added as he let go of her hand, "Are you from around here?"

"I'm from Los Angeles," he said. "But not Newport Beach, no."

"I was born and raised here. I think sometimes it shows."

"Not in a bad way, Keri."

She smiled. "What do you mean by that?"

"Oh." He scratched his head. "You don't look like a rich snob."

"No, I'm a poor one. Where are you from exactly?"

"Here and there." He turned back to the movies. "I don't stay in any one place very long."

"Really? How do you support yourself?" She paused. "I'm being nosy, sorry."

He smiled, almost as if to himself. "Not in a bad way."

She giggled. "But not in a good way, either, huh?"

He shrugged and picked up a video. "It doesn't matter." He held *The Wizard of Oz*. "What's your favorite line in this movie?" he asked.

"When the Cowardly Lion says, 'I do believe in spooks. I do believe in spooks.' What's your favorite line?"

"Pay no attention to the man behind the curtain."

"I should have guessed."

He was curious. "Why do you say that?"

She hesitated. "Because you look like the guy

behind the curtain." She added hastily, "Just kidding."

He stared at her. "How old are you?"

"Seventeen. Why? Do I seem older?"

"Yes."

"How old are you?"

"Twenty."

"You seem older." She giggled like a little girl. "Do we both have gray hair or something?"

"Something." He considered, *something,* then turned back to his movies. "It was nice to talk to you, Keri."

Was that it? He was cutting her off, and their conversation had started well. She wondered if she had offended him. Well, she wasn't someone to push herself on anyone.

"Take care of yourself, Oscar," she said, turning away.

"You, too, Keri," he said to her back.

She had to work till closing, eleven, and Oscar was long gone before then. In fact she never did see him leave. Not long after they spoke she had to go in the back, and when she came out he was gone. His departure made her feel sad because he had seemed like an interesting guy. She doubted that she would ever see him again. He lived here and there, he said—he got around.

Clay met her as she walked to her car. As he often did, he had been waiting in the parking lot for her. He practically jumped out of his car when he saw her, and hurried over. Clay had energy—it bubbled off his slightly pudgy cheeks and kept him from standing still for more than five seconds. The two times they had slept together, he had tossed and turned all night. Apparently he always did; his dream life must have been as intense as his waking state.

And Clay was intense. He made their relationship desperate—he clung to her as if she were the last life raft aboard the *Titanic*. Yet, ironically, he could be very friendly and patient. If she pushed him away, or appeared to do so, that was when he freaked out. But it was virtually impossible not to say something that would upset him. Because of her lousy job and miserable home life, she often had to spend most of her weekends studying just to keep up. She'd talked to him about it last week and he was hurt. Their Saturday night movie dates, in his opinion, were sacred, and now she was taking them away. She told him that they could still go out Saturdays, just not *every* Saturday. But he had taken their talk badly and had sulked all week at school. But now here he was, Friday night, and anxious to make amends. She knew that Clay lived in absolute terror of her leaving him, which was scary since she wanted to half the time.

Clay had many fine qualities, however. He was brilliant at math and science and computers. He also read tons of books and had a photographic memory. According to him he and she were the two smartest people in the school and naturally that meant they belonged together.

He wasn't bad looking, although he was putting on weight—his weight was a button she knew never to push. She couldn't even talk about her own random diets in his company. His hair was blond and short, his face round as an owl's. His large blue eyes were his best feature—he was only eighteen and already his eyes twinkled. He drank a dozen Dr. Peppers a day and loved jelly doughnuts. He was no way near obese, just soft around the middle, but when they had made love Keri was not excited and that worried her. She wasn't so superficial that bodies meant everything to her. Still, their sex had not come close to that in her fantasies.

Clay gave her a warm hug and she tried to return the gesture. Her fellow employees were getting off work, and she had warned him before not to try to kiss her in front of them. Not that she was close to anyone in the store. Clay let go of her and took a step back. He had on gray slacks and a freshly pressed white shirt. She wore blue jeans and a red sweater she had stolen from her mother. He usually dressed up a bit; she preferred to be casual. Of course his family had plenty of money, something he was always trying to give her. Clay was generous to a fault, but she made it a rule to let him pay for their dates and nothing else. She didn't use people or their money.

"How was work?" he asked.

"Not bad—the time went quick."

"So you're not tired?"

A leading question, she realized. He wanted her to come over to his place, where she knew she would have to wrestle with him for an hour. He was worried that they hadn't made love again, and again she cursed herself for having opened that door. Now she could no longer say she wanted to wait for marriage or something stupid like that. If the truth be known she was anxious to have sex, just not with him. There were other attractive guys at school who wanted to take her out. Then there was Oscar—damn how fast he had cut her off. She was still wondering what she had done wrong.

"I'm a little tired," she replied, yawning for effect. "What have you been up to tonight?"

"Went to the movies with Bob." Bob was his best friend, the official class nerd but a nice guy. Bob had thick glasses and zits and a mom who still drove him to piano lessons. Clay added, "We saw *Kill the Cop* by that new rap star Chrome Shoes. It was well written, a satire on ghetto violence. The audience clapped at the end. Some say it might get nominated for an Oscar."

"An Oscar would be nice," she muttered.

"Keri?" he asked.

"Nothing." She yawned again, this time for real. "I think I should go home and get to bed."

"I thought you weren't tired?"

"I didn't say that. Plus I need to get up early tomorrow and do errands."

"What do you have to do?" he asked.

"A bunch of stuff." She turned to her car door and took out her key. "Can I call you tomorrow?"

"Sure. But you don't want me to come over now?"

"No. You know my mom. She always saves up a

few grams for Friday nights. God knows what shape she'll be in."

"She'll probably be passed out. We can watch a little TV. I'll make popcorn."

"I'm sorry, Clay, I'm just not in the mood."

He studied her. "Is something wrong?"

"No."

"Then why don't you want me to come over?" he asked.

"I told you, I'm tired."

"You're not mad at me?"

"No."

"You sound mad."

"I'm not," she said.

He was unconvinced. "But it's Saturday tomorrow. You don't really have to be anywhere early. We can hang out for a while and you can still get enough sleep."

She sharpened her tone. "Clay?"

"What?"

"You're pushing. We talked about this, I don't like to be pushed."

He took a step back. "I want to hang out with my girlfriend. What's wrong with that?"

She almost said that she was not his girlfriend. The words were on her lips, perhaps he saw them forming, for his expression changed—a cloud on the horizon, no, a storm. Once they got to debating their relationship there was no stopping him. She reached out and took his hand and spoke gently.

"There's nothing wrong with that," she said. "I appreciate that you want to come over. I'm grateful that you waited for me to get off work. But I really am tired and I have a big day tomorrow. OK?"

He shrugged. "OK. But we're still going out tomorrow?"

"We'll see." She raised a hand to stop him. "Probably, I'm just not sure. Stacey asked if I could cover for her tomorrow night. I might do it—I need the money."

He shook his head. "But you never work Saturdays. I mean, I can give you the thirty or forty bucks."

"No."

"But—"

"No." She gave him a kiss on the cheek and got in her car. Rolling down her window, she leaned outside and squeezed his hand. "I'll call you tomorrow, I promise."

"Are you going straight to bed?" he asked.

"Yeah."

Not really. When she got home her mother was building a fire in the fireplace. It was so huge the logs—and the flames—were spilling onto the carpet. Keri figured another thirty minutes and her mom would have burned the building down. But maybe not, her mother liked to dance close to the flames but didn't really want to die. Keri suspected her behavior was an extended cry for help. The problem was that even when the cry was answered it made no real difference. Keri swiped the poker from her mother's hands and shoved two of the logs deeper into the fireplace. There was smoke in the barren room, flakes of ash drifting on the depressed air. They had a couch, a coffee table, and a lamp left, not much else.

"What are you doing?" Keri snapped.

Her mother smiled, an expression curious on her. Despite the drugs and her crazed eyes, she was still a beautiful woman. Taller than Keri, her mother had thick blond hair and a slender figure. Her smile was generous—Keri had been lucky to get her mom's mouth. It was perhaps in her voice that one heard the toll from the drugs. Even when her mom tried to act happy, she sounded depressed. Her tone was heavy when she giggled.

Such observations were all on the surface. Keri knew her mom's liver was beginning to fail. Seemed the body's old chemical factory didn't like processing unnatural quantities of super-refined coca leaves. Their family doctor—who had been a friend and still saw them for free—told her mom that if she didn't kick her habit she would need a liver transplant. Keri had chirped in something about a brain transplant. Her mom had been high at the doctor's office.

Like right now, her brown eyes were not merely shiny, they were radioactive. She laughed as Keri fought with the burning logs and lazily threw herself onto the couch.

"Just trying to keep warm, honey," she said.

"Have you heard of turning on the heat?" Keri asked angrily as she stamped out a spark on the carpet. The rug was a piece of junk but it was better than the petrified wood beneath it. Her mom, wrapped in an oversize gray robe, lay horizontal on the saggy couch and continued to chuckle.

"Have you heard of a bill not being paid and the heat being turned off?" she asked.

Keri dropped the poker on the bricks, it was hot.

"You're kidding?" she asked. "Is the stove off as well?"

"It's not an electric stove, Keri."

"Well, that's just great. How are we supposed to cook?"

"Who cares? We never cook. All you make is oatmeal in the morning."

Keri shoved her mother's legs aside and sat on the couch.

"I like oatmeal in the morning," Keri said coldly. "I like hot tea at night. I like houses that are not on fire. And I'd like a normal life and not worry each time I leave that my mother will be dead when I return."

Her mother lost her smile. "I'm not going back into rehab."

"Then what are you going to do? You can't live like this. *We* can't."

Her mother reached for a cigarette. "You're free to leave whenever you want. Marry Clay—he has money and he loves you."

"I'm seventeen years old and in high school, I can't get married. You're my mother, you're supposed to be telling me things like this, not the other way around."

Her mother lit her cigarette and took a puff and sighed.

"What's the point in talking about it? We'll just fight. I'm the way I am, I've accepted it."

"So you accept that you're a whore?"

Her mother did not snap at her as she expected but turned her head toward the fire. Keri thought she saw a tear in the corner of her mother's eye but could have been mistaken.

"I'm not a whore," her mother whispered.

Keri regretted the use of the word. "Can I get you something to eat? I picked up a pizza on the way home."

"I'm not hungry."

Her mother was never hungry. Cocaine was great for losing those extra inches, Keri thought. Maybe Clay should give it a try. Keri squeezed her mother's foot and stood.

"I'm not hungry, either," she said. "I'm going to bed."

"But what about the pizza?"

"We can eat it tomorrow."

Keri went into the bathroom and then undressed in her bedroom. Crawling under the blankets on her miserable mat and turning out her one remaining lamp, she thought of Oscar—his strange bony face, deep-set eyes, and soft voice. She had heard him speak before, somewhere, she was sure of it.

Maybe it had only been in a dream.

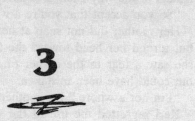

3

The next day, Saturday, she did take Stacey Mingle's shift. As a result she was back sorting CDs when Oscar paid another visit to the store. She saw him come in but didn't think he saw her. He immediately headed for the old movie section, and she left him alone for twenty minutes before summoning the courage to approach him. When he did see her he smiled slightly, his deep gray eyes shining. He wore white pants, a gray shirt, and a sports coat. The latter was slightly wrinkled but could have been made of cashmere.

"Keri," he said. "Seventeen, lover of old movies, poor."

She giggled. "You forgot born and raised in Newport Beach. How are you, Oscar? You watch all your movies already?"

"Yes."

She nodded to the black-and-whites. "What are you looking at now?"

"I'm not sure. I think I'm running out of choices."

"Then you might have to consider the color decades."

He paused. "I'm color-blind."

"Totally?"

"Yes."

"Isn't that rare?"

"I suppose."

"Well, it's not like you're blind."

"No."

"You can still watch color movies."

"That I can."

She tried to be casual. "I'm glad you came back."

He was curious. "Why?"

She was afraid he was going to ask that question. She shrugged. "I enjoyed talking to you yesterday. You're different from most of the guys who come in here."

"I'm grave?"

She smiled. "I wouldn't put it that way, but, yes, you're kind of serious."

"I'm sorry."

"No. I like that quality. It's refreshing. Hey, you never did tell me where you're from?"

He shrugged. "I have a place around here."

"What do you do? Work? School?"

"I work. I paint."

She was impressed. She had zero artistic ability and hated the fact.

"Do you make a living doing it?" she asked.

"Yes."

"That's great, I really admire that. I would do anything not to have to work in this crummy store."

He hesitated. "Would you?"

"Well, I wouldn't sell my body—not that anyone would pay for it. Yeah, but I've got to stay here. There's no money at home and I want to go to a halfway decent school next year. I'm looking at UCLA and USC."

"Good schools."

"Did you ever go to college?"

"Briefly."

"I guess it doesn't matter because you have talent. I mean, how can anyone teach you how to paint? What kind of art do you do?"

Another faint smile. "Black-and-whites."

She laughed. "Sure. What else? I would love to see your work sometime."

It was a strong hint—ask me out why don't you—and she waited with her heart pounding for him to respond. What shocked her, as he considered her remark, was how easily she had made a pass at him without thinking about Clay. The guilt, she was sure, would come later.

"If you want to see it," he said carefully, "I can show it to you. Most of it's at my place."

The ball was in her court. Should she volley it or smash it over the net? In other words, should she go for coffee with him or just let him make passionate love to her on one of his oversize canvases? Decisions, decisions—she did love coffee. Oh, but he was awfully interesting looking, so different from Clay. His soft voice was enough to send her into a different dimension, one of many colors.

"OK," she gushed.

He was puzzled. "OK?"

"Yeah, show me your stuff." She added, "When it's convenient for you, I mean."

He glanced around. "What time do you get off?"

"Eleven."

"Is that late for you?" he asked.

"No. I'm a night person. If you want to come back then, we can have coffee or something." She added, "It's up to you."

He nodded. "I can come back."

"You want to meet in the parking lot?"

"That would be fine."

"Wait." Clay might be in the parking lot. "Let's meet at the Starbucks down the street. It's open till midnight. I'll be there a few minutes after eleven."

He took a step toward the door. "I'll be there."

"Oscar?"

He paused. "Yes?"

"Don't you want to get a movie?"

A small grin. "Another time."

Boy, she felt jazzed. The rest of the evening passed slowly and quickly at the same time. She wished she was better dressed—the same jeans as yesterday, with a faded yellow blouse—but figured he wouldn't care. She wasn't sure who had asked whom out.

Clay was waiting, dear boy, she wanted to strangle him.

"We can catch a later movie at the Roxy," he said as he gave her his usual long and smothering hug. "They're showing that remake of *Invasion of the Saucers. The Times* said it wasn't bad. I already got us tickets."

"I can't go."

His chubby face deflated. "What? Why not?"

"I'm tired. I want to go home."

"But you were tired last night."

"Clay, it's eleven at night. What time does the movie start?"

"Twelve. We have time to get coffee and a muffin, that will wake you up. Let's go to Starbucks and order a double cappuccino."

"No!"

"Keri?"

She fought to calm herself. God, did she feel guilty, she hated lying to people, especially someone she was supposed to like. Her upbringing had done a number on her programming. Halfway through coffee with Oscar, she would probably tell him all about Clay.

"Let's go out tomorrow night," she said. "We'll go out early, and then go for a walk afterward."

He was interested. "Will you come over to my place afterward?"

"Maybe, if you behave yourself."

He sneered and moved in for a kiss. "You don't want me to behave. What fun is that?"

She kissed him quickly on the lips and then playfully pushed him away.

"We'll see," she said. "I'll call you in the morning."

"What time?"

"Nine-seventeen. I don't know, I'll call you."

"You promise?"

"I promise." She opened her car door and got in. "Take care."

He leaned in on her rolled-down window. "Call me when you get home. We can talk as you go to sleep. Remember how we used to do that all the time? It was so romantic."

"It was, but let's not do it tonight. I just want to sleep."

He took a step back as she started the car. "I'll call to make sure you got home all right."

"You don't have to."

"It's no problem," he said.

She decided she was making him suspicious, he wasn't stupid. She could always call from the Starbucks, warn her mother to say that she was asleep. Her mother was a good liar; most drug addicts were.

"Call then, but I don't promise to be awake," she said.

He wished her pleasant dreams, and she left the parking lot in the direction of home. Fortunately she had the jump on Clay, he wasn't able to follow her. At the next block she made a turn and went down a side street. In minutes she was at the Starbucks, but chose to stop to call her mother from a phone at an adjacent gas station. A glance inside the coffee shop had shown her that Oscar was already waiting.

Her mother didn't even ask why she was to lie; she simply told Keri not to worry about it. Keri set the phone down and went to check her face in the gas station bathroom. All she had in her purse was a lipstick and a roll of breath mints. She couldn't believe how flat her hair was; it was as if she had slept the night before on someone's floor—ha. For sure, she was not taking Oscar home to meet Sugar Mama. On the other hand he was a color-blind artist and a little spacey, maybe he did drugs himself. It would be just her luck.

He stood as she approached his table; she gestured for him not to bother. He had already ordered himself a cup of coffee and three large muffins—carrot, blueberry, and banana nut. Maybe it was his dinner, she thought as she watched him heap on the butter and wash the whole down with a large steaming coffee. He asked what she wanted and she said a double cappuccino, her usual. He was back in two minutes with her order. After buttering another muffin, he offered it to her. She shook her head no.

"I'm skinny but I need to eat a lot," he said, by way of apology. "Are you sure you don't want a muffin?"

"No. I have a problem with food."

"Which is?" he asked.

"When I eat I get fat."

He nodded as he took a bite of muffin. "I can't

42

gain weight, no matter how much I eat. It's my metabolism."

"I must get one of those." She sipped her coffee, loved how it burned her tongue. Good to get it raw and sensitive in case he wanted to kiss her. Her rush continued to percolate—it was exciting to be alone with him, in a crowded place. She added, "Were you waiting long?"

"No." He paused and caught her eye. "Why didn't you want to meet me at the video store?"

"This is a nice place to meet." She took a breath. "Don't you think?"

He relaxed his gaze; it could be intense when he cranked it up. She suspected there was more to Oscar than met the eye, and he was pretty complex even at first glance. She asked herself if it was wise to go to the apartment of a guy she barely knew, especially late at night.

"The muffins *are* good here," he agreed.

She shrugged. "It's just that I don't know much about you, and I'd rather meet in a public place."

He chewed. "You don't know *anything* about me, Keri."

She smiled quickly. "You seem like an interesting guy. Did you always paint?"

"No, I started last year."

"Wow. And you really sell your work?"

"Yes."

"You must have incredible talent."

"We all have talents—buried deep inside us."

"What sparked your creative outbursts?"

The question seemed to touch him. He glanced out the window.

"A girl," he said.

Choke on that, Keri, why don't you. But he was not trying to goad her.

"Are you still friends with her?" she asked carefully.

"No."

"What happened? I mean, you don't have to say."

He shrugged and picked at his muffin. "She was not really a friend, but she had a powerful effect on my life."

"Are you still in touch with her?"

"No."

"Was she an artist?"

"No." He took a large swallow of coffee and his eyes returned to her face. "But she knew how to get to a person." He added, "Let's not talk about her."

"OK." Fine with her. "Do you have many friends who live around here?"

"No. None, actually."

"So you haven't been here long?"

"I move around. You're a senior?" he asked.

"Yes. Another seven months and I'll be a real adult."

"What do you want to major in at college?"

"No idea. It always blows my mind when people my age do know what they want to do. Half the time I think they talk themselves into a major because society demands it."

"Society is full of demands," he said.

She sensed he was telling her something important about himself.

"But you feel you escaped those demands with your art?" she asked.

"No." He became thoughtful. "There are many ways to escape."

"But is that what you want to do? It sounds . . . immature."

"Maybe. But I think we all have the same desire. To be free."

She was not sure where he was headed. "Tell me about your family?"

He took another bite of muffin. "I have none."

"Not a single relative?"

"No. How about you?"

"Well, I live with my mom." She paused. "But she has bad problems."

"Tell me."

Two simple words—somehow they made her want to tell all. Yet, with the exception of Clay, she had never spoken of her problems with her friends at school. But she felt she could trust Oscar; she sensed his elusiveness was not manipulative. She had been wrong to hint at his immaturity—more and more she was sure he had gone through a lot in his life. Definitely he must have suffered a tragedy of some type.

So she told him about her parents, the divorce, the drugs, even the mat on the floor. He listened without interrupting, his deep gray eyes drinking in her face and words. Nothing she said surprised him.

When she was through he stared silently out the window.

"Who is helping you through this?" he asked finally, his tone far from prying.

She shrugged. "I have this boyfriend, sort of. But it's over between us. I just don't have the heart to tell him."

He nodded. "But you have to tell him."

"I know, I know." She hesitated. "How about you?"

He shook his head. "I'm a loner."

"Then why did you want to have coffee with me?"

He glanced at her. "Because you're a loner."

"I don't think of myself that way."

"It doesn't matter. It's there on your face." He smiled faintly. "Besides, you asked me out."

"No, I didn't. Well, not directly. Besides, I really do want to see your art."

He was quietly amused. "You will have to come to my place. Just you and me, no one to save you if I turn out to be dangerous."

She giggled. "You're not dangerous."

He stared. "I am not as I appear, Keri."

She went to his place, maybe she needed a little danger in her life, maybe she was just bored. He lived in a spacious condo on Balboa Island: security gates, high ceilings, a righteous view of the harbor—money all around. The soft lights came on automatically as they entered, his large black-and-white paintings staring down at her from the walls

46

like oversize invitations. What style did his work fit into? She would have been hard-pressed to answer. Abstract modern and twisted gothic—the painting by the door depicted a worried child staring at a gigantic steel ball rushing at him. Did Oscar see his innocence already crushed? There was another painting—all hard angles and shades of gray—of a cube-shaped man trying to pass through a round door.

The furniture was black and white as well. No color in the entire condo. What you can't see can't hurt you, Keri thought. She tried to imagine what he saw when he looked at her, or rather, she was afraid to imagine.

She walked around and studied his work. He stepped out on the balcony and watched the boats coming and going beside the jetty. She finally joined him, shivering in the night air.

"You're amazing," she said.

"I'm weird."

"Most geniuses are."

He shook his head. "I'm not a genius. I'm just . . . lost."

"How are you lost?" She gestured behind them. "You're a success, you have all this."

He stared again into her eyes, and she felt a momentary dizziness. A sensation of falling into a familiar place. Like his voice, she was sure, she had seen his face long ago. They were fleeting images, instantly wiped away.

Why was she so drawn to him?

"I am lost because I am alone," he said.

His seriousness made her self-conscious.

"You could have any girl."

"No."

"Why not? You're handsome, talented, nice, maybe rich."

"Rich." He sighed and turned back to the harbor. "Do you want to go out on my boat?"

"You have one?" How exciting.

"Yes." He gestured off to the left. "We have to walk around, but it's not far away. It's called *Quintalen*—a forty-foot powerboat. I take it out to Catalina occasionally and up and down the coast."

"I'd love to go out." She pointed to the eastern horizon. "It looks like the moon will be up soon."

"Moonlight on the water is nice," he agreed.

The *Quintalen* was only a minute away, all white and new, sleeker than she would have imagined, built for speed despite its three levels. Oscar held her hand as he led her onto the top deck that housed the control center. He left her there for a moment while he undid the lines, and then with a turn of the key and the powerful throb of the quiet engines, they were away. Surprisingly there were still boats coming and going through the harbor, but once out on the sea they were alone, the ocean ablaze with the glow of the half-moon. Oscar steered them straight out, then let the automatic navigator take over.

"The onboard computer is smart," he said. "It can be left to steer for hours. If we should approach another boat, it would steer around it."

"So you can set a course and go to sleep?" she asked.

"Yes."

"Do you ever do that?"

He paused. "Sometimes."

Almost without realizing what she was doing, she reached out and touched his long brown hair, stroked it, her fingers slowly sliding through the fine strands lit by the silver light. He watched her for a moment, then brought his head close. The kiss, when it happened, was a long slow affair. He was in no hurry to impress her, to consume her—rather, she felt savored. He tasted of love and loss, excitement and peppermints.

She held him and he touched her.

They ended up down below and she could not remember when she decided to make love to him. Perhaps the decision was his, but it wasn't as if he forced himself on her—nothing could be further from the truth. They took each other's clothes off in slow motion. Her earlier dizziness returned, and now she welcomed it because the strangely whirling tornado of her infatuation was lifting her high. He was right, she wanted to escape, with him, into a far-off realm where there were just the two of them and nothing to do but hold each other.

The waves gently rocked the boat, his naked body slid onto the bed beside her. His gray eyes silently said a million things to her. Only his unspoken words were in alien code. Had they not been, she would have immediately understood that he was not human. Had he muttered one line about what was on his mind, she would have fled screaming from the cabin and into the cold water if necessary—anything to escape what he had planned for her. But even when they lay together afterward and she dozed in his arms, she didn't notice his eyes on her, the watching, the waiting, the inscrutable longing masked only by deep dispassion. No, Keri Weir did not understand that she had just made love to death itself.

4

When she got home at dawn, Clay was waiting for her in his car. It would be an understatement to say he was upset. Even though he was parked across the street from her apartment complex, she didn't notice him until she was at her front door and fumbling with her key. Her mother always used all the locks; somebody might steal her nasal spray. Of course her mother probably wasn't home yet either. Keri knew her mother wouldn't be worried about her being out late.

Such could not be said for Clay. She jumped when he moved up to her. Tears streamed down his face—he looked as if he had spent the night in a garbage truck. She wondered how she was going to lie to him. No good excuse came to her in the two seconds he gave her to respond.

"Keri," he cried. "Where have you been?"

She dropped her keys and had to pick them up. She shrugged. "I was out."

"Where?"

She swallowed. "I was, well, out with Cindy."

His face fell farther, if that was possible. "I drove by Cindy's house. She was home all night, you weren't with her. Keri, why are you lying to me?"

It was a reasonable question. "I was out with a guy."

He fought to breathe. "What guy?"

"This guy I met at the store."

He was close to a heart attack. "Who is he?"

"Clay . . ."

"How long have you been seeing him?"

"I saw him for the first time tonight . . . last night."

He shook. "But why were you out all night with him?"

She averted her eyes. "I don't know."

He moaned. "Keri! Did you sleep with him?"

"No, of course not." She paused. "It's no big deal, really. Go home and rest. You don't have to worry about him."

When she tried to open her door, he grabbed her arm and turned her around. His face was so contorted with grief and anxiety that she hardly recognized him. He had not merely aged during the night—he had started to decompose. She wanted to tell him the truth and end it now, but knew it would kill him. She figured that later would be better to explain—later was almost always better in situations like this, she thought, even though she had no experience with such situations, and hoped to have none in the future.

"You owe me an explanation," he said coldly as he continued to grip her arm. "You're not brushing me off."

She couldn't meet his gaze. "All right, come in then."

Inside, lying on the floor in her bathrobe with blood pouring out of her nose was her mother. The woman's eyes were open and she was still breathing, but not much else was going on. Keri dropped her bag and knelt beside her.

"Mom!" she cried, taking her wrist and finding a faint pulse. It was *so* slow—only twenty beats a minute. From beside her, Clay picked up a Baggie of white powder and tasted it.

"This isn't cocaine," he said.

"Sure it is," Keri said. "It's the only thing she puts up her nose."

"No. It's heroin."

"How do you know?"

"I know."

She didn't argue—when Clay was positive about something, he was always right. He had partial knowledge about practically everything. She slapped her mother lightly on the face but got no reaction. Her mother's glazed eyes were fixed on the ceiling.

"Is she going to die?" she asked.

"She's overdosed, but a hospital can save her."

He stood. "I'll call the paramedics. Keep trying to stimulate her."

"How?"

"Pinch her, shake her. Keep talking to her."

For the next ten minutes Keri did her best, but with no results. Her mother's breathing became labored—Keri had to put her head to her mom's chest to be sure her heart was still beating. Clay kept rubbing and shaking her mom's legs. Keri knew if her mom choked she wouldn't have enough life left to clear her lungs. Clay rolled the woman onto her side in case that happened.

The paramedics were there in ten minutes and off they went to the hospital, Keri and Clay chasing the ambulance in his car. He never brought up the previous night, and for that she was grateful.

"Why would she snort heroin?" she mumbled as they sped through a red light.

"She probably didn't do it intentionally."

"What do you mean?"

"You hinted that she was 'working' for her pusher. He might have gotten mad at her for some reason and wanted to punish her. Gave her heroin instead of cocaine."

"She should have been able to tell the difference."

"Not necessarily."

"She's a goddamn expert when it comes to drugs."

"Nobody is an expert on anything when they're high."

He had a point. Minutes later, at the hospital,

the doctors confirmed that what was in the Baggie was largely heroin—high-grade stuff, too. They weren't sure they could save her. Keri's last glimpse of her mother, before she was wheeled away, was of a nurse slipping a ventilator over her face. Another nurse told them to sit and relax. It would be hours before they'd know which way it would go.

Relax—what a word for a time like this. Yet as Keri slumped in a chair beside Clay, her head cradled in the hollow of his shoulder, she felt a profound weariness pass over her. Her own mother was fighting for life, but try as she might Keri could not fight off sleep. It was pressed upon her from the outside, from another time even, and the dream it produced was like a vision forced into her cranium.

A garden. A place for souls to go at the end of life. Paradise filled with warmth and light—enchanted nature stretching for endless miles.

Yet the light was so bright, the temperature so warm, that perhaps paradise had been miscalculated by inches. It didn't matter to her, though, one place was the same as another. She was Keri Weir and she was something else. The all-encompassing white light pierced the trees and flowers, the grass and streams, blurring distinctions—as her indifference also did. She remembered being human but memory was not reality. Not totally without feeling, a faint sense of curiosity and of discontent stayed with her.

She stood on a wide lawn beside a vast lake, trees

and hills climbing up behind the lake. The water was warm and still, a mirror. She was naked but it didn't bother her because those around her were unclothed as well: beautiful specimens that could have been mistaken for humans, three dozen or so, their faces calm, only their eyes alert. They languished beside the lake, took walks in the hills, spoke quietly among themselves, let time pass. They knew her, she was one of them, but she was separate from them as well because they did not share her discontent. They were not predisposed to share anything.

It seemed, in that realm, as if time itself were a disease. Nothing ever changed, time was endless. There was no pain but no joy either—tranquility and beauty did not entertain, not her at least. As she walked along the lake, ran her hands through the clean water and picked the fragrant flowers, her discontent shadowed her—a paradox when there was so much light. Yet her unease did not grow strong enough for her to seek a cure. Time flowed like one of the streams that fed the lake, and she could not imagine what could stop it. Her immortality was a curse and a blessing—all things, she assumed, were that way.

One day, though, she noticed a line of darkness on the distant horizon. The others noticed it as well, she saw them point at it and speak of it among themselves. But their conversations were subdued, as lively as the easy breeze, and she knew they would not explore it. The darkness was like a cloud—it hung above the most distant hill. All day it remained, and it seemed to grow. To reach it she would have to walk far and climb high hills, but it tugged her forward. Finally she began to walk toward it, and the others watched her go without comment. They didn't care if she ever returned.

The day wore on—it was never truly night in that realm—and she continued her hike toward the dark cloud. For the first time in a while she knew strain and fatigue. The terrain was steep and the ground changed from soft grass to hard rock and sand. Her feet slipped as she climbed, and she had to lean forward and press hard with her legs. The effort to keep going intimidated her, and many times she wanted to stop and turn around. What kept her going were vague memories, of being on earth, of the name Keri Weir. For it seemed the more she sweated the more she recalled her previous life. Still, it was the memory of a dream—she no more believed in the past than she did in the future. In that place—maybe it was hell, maybe heaven—both were identical. But the journey toward the darkness had sparked something inside her, and she knew she would not rest until she reached it.

The final hill, around which the cloud had gathered, was more mountainlike, covered with black stone and thick ash. Living beside the lake, she could never have imagined that such a place existed. She wondered if the cloud itself had turned the area black. Far above her she spotted the source of the cloud—a wide cave from which dark smoke poured. There was no smell, no change in temperature, and the smoke did not cause her to cough. But as she continued to hike toward it opposites grew in her mind—she was drawn to and repulsed by the cave. She felt that if she were to enter it everything she knew would change, and not necessarily for the better. Yet she was still attracted to it and realized how tired she had grown of the light, at least the cave offered change, something to break the endless monotony.

Just before the cave entrance she saw a figure naked and pale standing on a smooth black stone. His gaze was fixed on the smoke pouring out of the cave, but he turned as she neared and she recognized him. Oscar . . . yes, that was what he called himself, once a long time ago, although she knew that he had another name. His gray eyes stared at her with sorrow, and she wondered if his proximity to the cave had stamped it on his expression. Definitely, the cave was a place of power, and she couldn't understand why he hadn't entered it. But as she framed the question in her mind he shook his head and gestured for her to continue without him. For some reason he could go no farther, and the realization brought with it a sense of loss. She cared for Oscar, she remembered. Keri Weir had loved him.

Inside the cave the smoke was so dense she could see nothing. Yet just when all light was extinguished she saw a faint glow up ahead. The smoke poured over her like an etheric current—largely without substance—as she strode quickly toward the light. It took on the shape of a rectangle, a door. A dark shape stood at its center. The white light that flared here was unlike the light she had known beside the lake. This light was dynamic, it moved and frightened her at the same time. A cold wind blew through that open door and a chill surrounded the presence that stood before her. Still, it was only a silhouette, one of a tall man with long thick hair. He had no face, no voice. She knew he had been waiting for her for a long time.

She stopped before the man and the smoke cleared. Yet the light behind him made her half blind. The man moved like an animated shadow that grew and stretched across the doorway. He moved casually, without impatience, waiting for her. She felt both terror and wonder—it was good to feel at all, she realized. That was why she had traveled so far. A part of her had known what she would find. Yet mystery dominated.

"Who are you?" she asked.

His reply was in the voice of an angel, the whisper of a devil. There was no humanity in his tone, yet it gave her the impression that he understood humans. The reply was gentle and confusing.

"Does it matter?" he said.

"To me, yes. Who are you?"

"It does not matter."

"No?"

"Do not panic."

"What do you want?"

"What do you want?" he asked.

"To understand. Did you bring me here?"

"No. Yes. You brought yourself here."

"Do you want something from me?"

"No. Yes. To ask you a question."

"What is this question?"

"Should I come?"

"Should you come?"

"Yes. Should I come?"

"Where?"

"To you. To them."

"I don't understand. You are with me now."

"No."

"Where would you come? Who are they?"

"It does not matter. Do not panic."

"What does matter?"

"The question. Should I come?"

"What is your purpose?"

"You would not understand."

"Are you good? Evil?"

"They do not apply."

"Why do you ask me this question?"

"It is your decision."

"Why is it my decision?"

"You have been chosen."

"Why?"

"You stand between light and dark."

"I don't understand."

"It does not matter."

"If you come what will happen?"

"Nothing will ever be the same. But do not panic."

"Why do you stand in this door?"

"I did not make it."

"Who did make it?"

"It does not matter."

60

"Why can't I see your face?"

"It is not yet time."

"But will I see your face?"

"No. Yes. Should I come?"

She hesitated. "Yes. Come."

There was a long pause.

It could have been eternal.

"You will see my face," he said.

"Keri," someone said. "Wake up, the doctor wants to talk to us."

Keri opened her eyes and felt a stabbing pain in her neck. If not for the pain and Clay saying her name it would have taken her longer to know *who* she was. Waking up was completely disorienting—half of her soul still felt trapped in that strange dream. The voice of the man in the doorway faded slowly, a figure sinking below the surface of a cold lake. Sitting up, she blinked several times and put a hand to her head.

"What time is it?" she mumbled.

"Ten o'clock, you've been asleep for four hours," Clay said.

Keri came instantly awake. "How's my mom?"

Clay stood and offered his hand. "A nurse was just here; we have to go talk to the doctor. But I think the news is good."

A wave of relief washed away her physical discomfort. She let Clay help her up and followed him down the hall to an office. Presently a young doctor appeared, clad all in green scrubs—the guy looked as if he had pulled a twenty-four-hour shift. Despite his fatigue, he had a commanding air. He briefly shook their hands, then sat down on a chair beside them.

"Your mother is going to be OK," he said to Keri. "The crisis has passed. All her signs are stable. But its obvious from examining her that she has a serious drug problem and that she won't be OK if she doesn't receive help. To be blunt, she will die, and not too far in the future." He paused. "From your expression I suspect I'm not telling you anything you don't already know."

Keri nodded. "But she doesn't want help. That's the problem—no clinic works unless a person wants to get better."

"It's possible this scare will motivate her," Clay said.

The doctor nodded. "We can hope for that. I'm really not an expert in this field. I can give you the numbers of people who are experts, though. I want her to remain in the hospital for today and tonight. This is largely precautionary, but I must insist on it." He stood. "I wish you both luck with this. I'm sorry I have to run. I have other patients."

She and Clay stood and shook the doctor's hand.

"Thanks for your help," Keri said sincerely. "Can we talk to her now?"

"Come back in a few hours," the doctor said. "She's sleeping now and I want her to rest as long as possible. An overdose like she just went through is a terrible trauma." The doctor headed for the door. "Take care."

"Thanks," Clay called after him.

They were alone together. They stared at each other.

"I'm sorry, Clay," Keri said softly.

He shrugged. "I'm happy I could be there for you at this time."

"No. I'm sorry about last night."

He took her hand. "We can talk about it in the car."

Outside, driving in the bright sunlight, Keri noticed a peculiar coolness in her lower abdomen. It was accompanied by vague cramps, uneasy pulses that came and went, yet it was nowhere near her period. She wondered if it was from all the sex. Oscar and she had made love six times—it could have been eight. His stamina had amazed her, his ability to give her pleasure. She had never imagined that sex could be so intoxicating. It had been like an endless ride that had a fresh surprise at every turn. Better than ice cream and chocolate—hands down. His hands . . . ah, they were as sensitive as they were elegant. The only problem was that the sex had not been with her boyfriend—Freud's old forbidden love syndrome, nothing added more spice.

"I guess one of us should say something," Clay remarked when five minutes of silence had elapsed.

"I should be the one," Keri muttered.

"Do you really like this guy?"

"Yeah, I really do."

Clay's lower lip trembled and he continued to stare straight ahead. He was controlling himself and she was proud of him for that, and she was grateful for his help with her mother.

"Are you going to see him again?" he asked.

"I think so. I want to."

"May I ask his name?"

"Oscar. I don't know his last name."

"Where does he live?"

"Balboa. He has a condo there. It's on the water."

"Nice. How old is he?"

"Maybe twenty, I'm not sure. He paints for a living."

"Is he good?"

"Yeah, he's good."

Her tone must have betrayed her thoughts. He glanced over.

"This is none of my business—" he began.

"It is your business," she interrupted. "I lied to you. I did sleep with him." She reached for his arm. "I'm so sorry. You don't deserve this."

Clay had to take a few deep breaths, but he managed to stay on the road. He had to know already. Who stayed out all night and had coffee? She reached over to put a hand on his arm and felt it tremble, but he kept his grief in check.

"I guess it's over between us then," he said.

"Yeah. It's over." She paused. "I don't want to sound like a cliché and say we can still be friends. I'm sure you don't even want to talk to me right now. But later, when things smooth out—if they do for you—I would like to be your friend. I know my actions last night don't show it, but I have a lot of respect for you, Clay."

"I'll need some time." He considered. "I'm worried about this guy, though."

"You don't have to worry."

"I suppose I sound a little possessive, but it doesn't sound like you know much about him."

"I agree. He's something of a loner."

Clay swallowed. "Did you tell him about me?"

"I did, yes. He wanted to know."

"That was decent of him."

"He's a nice guy. He told me I had to end it with you to be with him."

Clay shook his head. "And you just met him, wow."

She stroked his arm. "Sometimes it happens like that. But what the hell do I know? I could have been a one-night stand for him. We both might end up dumped." She stopped herself. "I'm sorry, I shouldn't have used that word."

"It's a good word." Clay looked over. "I'd take you back."

"Really?"

"I would," he said.

"Please don't think about doing that. Better we call it quits. That way it's clear and you can move on. I don't want to get your hopes up."

"You always fill me with hope, Keri."

"You don't need me and I don't deserve you. Not now."

"All right." He sighed. "But we sure had some good times, didn't we?"

She let go of his arm and stared out the window.

"Sometimes good times aren't enough," she said.

5

There was nothing more to discuss, she hoped. When she got home, she gave Clay a hug and told him to stay in touch. He was quiet—the poor guy, she really had dumped him hard. Inside her apartment she took a shower—a cold shower, no gas, remember—before popping a couple of Tylenol. The cramps in her abdomen had not worsened, but they hadn't gone away either. The cold from the shower did nothing to wake her up. She continued to feel drowsy and stretched out on her mat for a short nap.

When she awoke it was dark.

She had slept away the entire day.

The phone was ringing. It must have awakened her.

"Hello?" she said as she pulled herself into a sitting position.

66

"How did I get here?" her mother asked.

"You know how you got there," Keri said flatly. "You scared the hell out of me. How do you feel?"

"Great. I slept all day." Her mother paused. "You found me?"

"Clay and I did, yeah. It wasn't a pretty sight."

"I bet, my nose is all bandaged. How close was it?"

"Real close. Mom, you have to stop. You have to promise me. I can't take this, no one could."

Her mother sighed. "I promise I'll try."

"Do you really mean it?"

"I do." Her voice tightened and Keri heard tears, something her mother never gave in to. It gave Keri reason to hope. "I'm lying to you, you know. I'm not great, I'm scared."

"That's good. Scared is what you should be." Keri paused. "Do you want me to come down to the hospital?"

"Not tonight." Her mother coughed. "I think I'm going back to sleep."

"Call me if you change your mind. I should be here."

"Where were you last night? With Clay?"

"No. We broke up."

Her mother hesitated. "You amaze me, Keri."

"I amaze myself sometimes. Rest."

They exchanged goodbyes and Keri set the phone down.

It rang a few seconds later—Oscar.

"Do you want to get together tonight?" he asked.

"Sure. If you want to." She added, "I had a great time last night. I love your boat."

"It's a nice toy. We can go out on it again if you like."

"I'd love it." And other things. "Do you want to pick me up? Or should I drive down there? I don't mind."

He was silent a moment. "It would be easier for me if you came here. I'm in the middle of something. I need an hour or so to finish it. What time is it?"

She checked. "Eight-thirty."

"Why don't you come at ten, if that's not too late for you."

"No, that's fine. I rested a lot today."

"Good." He paused. "I'll see you then."

"Great!"

The initial rush was back, stronger. Her remark to Clay had not been idle—she was afraid she wouldn't hear from Oscar again. Not that she thought he was a jerk, he was simply . . . mysterious. Too elusive for a boring Orange County girl like herself. She had to caution herself that it still might not last. That girl in Oscar's past, the one who had opened him up—whatever the hell that meant—she felt something was still going on there. Tonight she had to learn his last name and where he was from. She couldn't screw a total stranger, after all.

Keri got up and took another cold shower. They were almost unbearable but what choice did she have? She took extra care with her long brown hair, blow drying it layer by layer. Fortunately she had so few clothes she didn't have to stress over what to wear. She settled on a pair of tan chinos and a white blouse. Last Christmas her father had given her a yellow cashmere sweater, and she put that on over her blouse. The entire process took close to an hour and it was time to go. Her car was parked out back, in the alley, in a crummy carport. She was uneasy about coming home late at night. Often homeless people hung out in the alley, and a few times they had startled her.

It was dark in the alley as she opened her car door.

She glanced around but didn't see anyone.

But *someone* . . . was there.

Keri heard no warning sound, he was simply there, behind her, putting a hand and a medicine-smelling cloth over her mouth. His other arm went around her chest and gripped her with bearlike strength—he actually raised her off her feet. Her legs kicked uselessly as she struggled. Terror momentarily blew all reason from her mind—except when it came to the cloth over her mouth. She could not identify the drug, but knew that if she breathed in the odor would knock her out. Then God knew what this beast would do to her.

She struggled, slashing back repeatedly with her elbows, trying to connect with his face. Several times she caught him in the jaw, but he only tightened his grip. His strength was unnatural—with all her fighting she hardly budged an inch. It was mostly her head that she tried to jerk free. If she could just get out a single scream, the neighbors might come to save her. But the guy knew what he was doing; he didn't so much as let her get out a moan.

Finally she had to breathe. The fumes from the drug flooded her nostrils and mouth. The taste was oddly sweet, vanilla and cough syrup. A numbing finger pushed deep into her brain. Her eyes closed, she could not keep them open. She felt her limbs go slack, realized vaguely that she had stopped struggling. From far away, it seemed, she heard feet being dragged across the pavement of the alley. She was drugged but not unconscious. She knew he was taking her to his car, to his castle, to put her naked on a tortuous rack and force her to confess. Yes, she was a witch, she had slept with Oscar when Clay was her boyfriend. Burn me at the stake; Satan will come for my soul.

She heard a car door open, felt a cloth sack being slipped over her head. With a supreme act of will she managed to open her eyes for an instant and saw that she was being covered with a pillowcase. She saw the car, a blur of blue, but the pillowcase was in place and she was falling forward over the front seat. The drug poked her brain cells with demon forks and she blacked out.

When she awoke next she was still in the car. The engine was running; they were going somewhere fast. Her head was still foggy, but she was awake enough to know her wrists and ankles had been bound with duct tape. The pillowcase around her head also felt tighter—there was a knotted string around her neck. She could breathe but that was all. Her heart pounded in her head—she realized her face was on the floor, her butt up in the air. She couldn't scream because her mouth was taped as well.

He put a hand on her butt. She felt him pull down her slacks; she wasn't wearing underwear. Horror filled her head with greater force than any drug. He was going to rape her and then he was going to kill her. He pinched her left cheek; his fingers were strong, the goddamn pervert, how could he do this to her? She felt a sharp stab, it could have been a needle. A peculiar numbness spread across her butt, and he pulled her trousers back up.

She was sure he had given her a shot to knock her out, but she remained alert, not believing what was happening to her. She couldn't be a news item; terrible things only struck strangers on the tube. She'd wake up soon, the cops would appear, Superman would swoop down and carry her off into the clouds. Then, for some reason, she thought of the dark figure in her nightmare. Should I come?

The car slowed and turned off the freeway onto surface streets. They turned left and right, her face still smashed into the floor. It got very quiet, and she couldn't imagine where they were or how long she had been unconscious. The car suddenly stopped and the driver turned off the engine. Her heart shrieked in her chest. Now he would rape her, now he would cut her, now she would bleed. He climbed out of the car and shut his door. He opened hers a moment later and pulled her head-first from the car.

Yet he didn't handle her roughly. Indeed, he picked her up in his arms rather gently and kicked the car door shut with his foot. She didn't struggle; it was now her strategy to pretend she was unconscious and to wait for an opening to escape. She couldn't die, she was only seventeen. Carrying her extra weight didn't appear to bother him; he walked quickly and with purpose. Straining her ears told her little. She heard cars moving, grumbling voices, doors opening and closing—all distant, all of no use to her. Yet she was sure she was still in the city and that gave her a measure of hope. Had he driven her to the desert, he would surely have buried her there.

Her hope faded a minute later.

They passed through a series of doors—she wasn't exactly sure how he opened them—and then the temperature suddenly fell. Not by ten or twenty degrees—they had entered arctic conditions. To be exact, he had taken her into a freezer of some type. Without ceremony, he set her down on the floor, frost crunching under her back. He did not stop to touch her or to speak. He turned and walked away, slamming a heavy door. All was still.

And cold, bitterly cold. The temperature was not merely below freezing, it was below zero. How long would her heart continue to beat in such cold? An hour? She would be completely numb long before then. Already she could feel the ice seeping into her butt and arms. Her blood would turn to cherry

72

snowflakes and clot her pink Popsicle brain. She had to get the tape off her ankles and wrists. She had to move!

Keri rolled on to her back and then decided to keep rolling. Her hands were bound in front of her. Anything sharp, preferably metal, would cut through the tape. She hadn't rolled far when she banged into boxes, possibly filled with vegetables and ice cream, in a grocery store freezer. Such frozen goods usually were stacked on pallets. Her wrists and hands were taped, but the tips of her fingers remained free. Unfortunately, they were the part of her body that was going numb fastest. Keri understood that if she did not free her hands in the next five minutes, she would die. The equation was that simple.

There was a pallet beneath the boxes and fortune favored her. The edge of the pallet was splintered and grooved. Pressing close to it she moved her taped hands up and down against the splintered edge. The tape made a faint squeaking sound, but because she couldn't see she wasn't sure if she was making any progress. A couple of minutes went by, and the feeling in her fingers decreased to a dangerous level. Panic swept over her, and she considered rolling to the other side of the room to find something metallic. But then she realized she wouldn't be able to feel it if she found it. Her fingers had lost practically all feeling; her hands would go next and the story would end.

Then she felt the tape give. Her hands popped apart an inch at the wrists, and she scraped at the sharp pallet with renewed enthusiasm. Another minute and she was able to pull her hands apart and tear the adhesive from her skin. After yanking the pillowcase off her head, she set to work on her feet. He had not bound them as tightly as her hands and soon she was free and standing up, trying to pound and slap feeling into her limbs. Her shivers were worse than convulsions.

She had gained maybe thirty minutes, but death was still close. The frozen blackness was patient. She could do jumping jacks all night to keep her flesh as warm as possible, but still the icy blackness would kill her. Her assailant had been clever enough to remove the safety ax from the back of the freezer door, which by law should have been waiting on its hooks to help her break out. Pounding furiously on the door and screaming at the top of her lungs brought no results. The door to the freezer was thick; her cries probably sounded muffled two feet outside the freezer. Plus her kidnapper had surely chosen a store that was closed and empty. She wondered why he had chosen this form of murder.

She wondered who he was.

Could he be waiting to come back for her? Really, why go to all this trouble to kill her? She briefly entertained the idea that he was simply trying to scare her, that the door would burst open and he would be waiting for her with a pot of steaming coffee. Fear had made her overly optimistic—ridiculously desperate was a better term. As her feet and hands started to go numb, she understood that escape was not an option. Jumping up and down and swinging her arms was not working because try as she might she could not stay on her feet. The ice was already well up her legs, past her knees; even her elbows creaked with frost. To sit down was madness, she knew, but the temperature brought her to the floor. She sat with her back against a pallet of frozen goods—the cold moved into her head.

"Oh God, help me!" she cried. Her tears, as they slid over her cheeks, turned to ice. It was so utterly black inside the freezer that it didn't matter if she closed her eyes, and yet it devastated her to do so because she knew she would never open them again. They would find her in the morning, the store employees. Or perhaps her assailant would come back for her after she was dead and eat her liver with fava beans, and a glass of chianti for contrast. In *Silence of the Lambs* Hannibal Lechter did that to innocent young women.

Oscar probably wondered where she was.

How cruel to find love only to lose it in death.

The cold continued to press down on her. She lost her feet and legs, her hands and arms. Her shivering began to subside and paradoxically was replaced by a warmth that spread through her abdomen and into her chest. It was as if hot thick liquid were being pumped into her blood from some mysterious inner source. She half expected to regain the use of her limbs, but then began to understand that the warmth was an illusion—death's graceful touch when embracing a freezing victim. She was not gaining heat, she was losing it so fast that her nervous system's response to the cold was numb.

She was dying. So unfair.

A corpse at seventeen.

"Oscar," she whispered. "Save me."

Those were her last words, as a human. Her last thought was of his face. She remembered, finally, where she had seen it before. A year ago in a newspaper, a black-and-white photograph. She couldn't recall all the details of the article, but they had been tragic. She remembered he was supposed to be dead as well.

6

Keri sat on her older sister's bed, in their old house, and watched as Debra removed clothes from the closet and chest of drawers and carefully folded them and put them in a large white suitcase. Yellow sunlight shone through the open window and a faint breeze—thick with the salt of the nearby ocean—caressed Keri's skin. Keri wasn't sure if it was a Sunday—it felt like a Sunday, lazy and carefree—but she knew she was back before the bad times. Back before her sister got cancer and died and her father had run away with another woman and left her and her mom. Keri was happy to be in the old house with Debra.

Her sister stopped packing and looked down at her. They looked nothing alike. Debra was two years older and had short blond hair and a full figure. Her eyes were like their dad's, green, and her nose was long and narrow, making the rest of her face—in contrast—appear soft. Yet Debra was very pretty, Keri had always thought so. Keri was pleased to see her so healthy, but was unsure about the expression that now crossed her sister's face.

"You shouldn't be here," Debra said.

"Why not?" Keri asked.

"You shouldn't be hanging out with me. You know why."

Keri felt a chill, but she couldn't remember what her sister referred to, or rather, she preferred not to. Still, she knew it would come to her in a minute.

"Why are you packing?" Keri asked, changing the subject.

Debra resumed putting clothes in the suitcase.

"Because I'm going away," she replied. "But before I do I need to talk to you about that guy you're dating. I tried to talk to you the other night, but you wouldn't listen."

"I don't remember that," Keri said.

Debra waved her hand. "It was when you were asleep. That's usually the only time I can talk to you. Anyway, I was telling you that you had to get away from that guy." She paused and stared. "But since you're here, I guess it's too late for that now."

"What do you mean?"

"You shouldn't be here, not now."

"I don't know what you mean." Again, Keri wanted to change the subject. "Don't you want to take your red sweater with you? The one I bought for your birthday last year?"

"You didn't buy that for me last year. That was three years ago." She set down the underwear she was holding and stepped to the bed and sat down beside Keri. "We really need to talk. I can't stay here long and I can't help you anymore."

Keri paused. "How have you been helping me?"

"I've been giving you advice. Not that you listen to it. Your head is so full of chatter that it's hard to get a word in edgewise. I'm like your guide, your guardian angel." She paused. "I'm dead, Keri, don't you remember?"

Keri giggled nervously. "No, if you're dead, how can I be talking to you?"

Debra took her hand and spoke firmly. "Enough of the BS. You know I'm dead and you know my death was the main reason Dad left and Mom started doing drugs. You don't like to think about it and you're usually successful at not thinking about it. But we've got serious stuff to talk about now and you've got to drop the denial. I tell you, I don't have time for it. OK?"

Keri was silent a moment. Her sister looked so real.

"I'm dreaming," she said finally. "You're just a product of my subconscious. I'm talking to myself."

Debra snorted. "That's true as well. The subconscious is big territory. I don't care how you look at it as long as you listen."

"OK," she said. "What do you need to tell me?"

"That guy you've been dating, he's roped you into a tight corner. The fact that you're here talking to me should tell you a lot."

Keri vaguely remembered the freezer.

"What did he do to me?" Keri asked.

"It's hard to explain, but you'll find out eventually. Enough to say it was weird, and now you're weird—neither dead or alive."

Keri chuckled. "Come on, Debbie. You cut the BS."

Debra shook her head. "I'm telling you straight, sis. You're in a difficult place right now. You should have listened to your heart. You knew the guy wasn't normal. You were just so lonely and horny that you went ahead and slept with him."

"Hey. You slept with a guy when you were alive."

Debra shrugged. "Yeah, I slept with a few."

"A few? Who did you sleep with besides Mark Cantor?"

"Gregory Bennet and Mike Field."

"You slept with Mike? I had a crush on him. You never told me."

Debra shook her head. "It doesn't matter. When you're dead, no one asks about how much sex you had while you were on Earth. Besides, none of those guys did to me what that guy did to you, and that's only half the problem. Because you had sex with him before he changed you, you've opened a door into a place that hasn't been opened in thousands of years."

"I don't know what you're talking about."

Outside, it seemed, the sun went behind a cloud. The temperature in the room dropped a few degrees, and Debra glanced around uneasily.

"I don't know how much I'm allowed to say," she said.

"What's the matter?"

Debra stood suddenly. "His influence reaches even here. I don't think he wants me to talk about him."

"Who is he?"

"It's hard to explain. He's the one you invited to come."

"I did? When?"

It suddenly grew very dark and cold. The walls of the bedroom seemed to move in, and Keri was reminded of the freezer she had been locked in. It all happened so fast—as if a winter cloud had blanketed the house. Even as she stared at her sister the light faded until the room was lit by nothing more than her sister's waning radiance. Debra's aura was a poor weapon against the dark cloud—it seemed to have a life of its own—a power stronger than anything the living or the dead could muster. Keri remembered the black smoke pouring out of the cave at the top of the mountain. Should I come? he had asked.

She had told him that he could.

"Why did you tell him that?" Debra asked as she began to fade from view.

Keri stood. Now she herself was cold, but it seemed to have no effect on her. Her flesh registered the low temperature as a rock might. She realized that there was no light left in the room, but she could see—in black and white. That was how it would be from now on. Her sister was only a shadow with large gaps; the white suitcase had vanished. They had only moments left together.

"I told him because he said his coming would bring change," Keri explained.

"But you didn't know who he was."

"How could I? You don't know who he is."

Her sister frowned as she faded to a faint outline.

"Certain things can't be explained," she whispered.

"Tell me what to do?" Keri pleaded.

"I don't know. You could try to kill yourself. At this point, that might be best."

"But I'll go to hell!"

Her dead sister shook her head sadly before she vanished.

She spoke but Keri did not hear what she said.

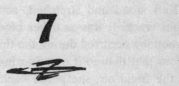

7

Keri awoke where she had blacked out. She assumed it was the same place but couldn't be sure where she had been before. Yet now there was a faint silver light in the freezer—radiating off the frozen cauliflower, glowing above the cartons of ice cream—and she could distinguish where she was in the room. She wondered briefly if someone had come to rescue her. But there was no sign of anyone, and as she sat listening she could hear no sounds other than the hum of the motor that drove the freezer compressor. It was odd but she hadn't noticed it before.

Oddness abounded. She was wide-awake and knew she had lost consciousness while freezing to death. The temperature was still below zero—her flesh registered that fact—but the cold did not trouble her. How was that possible?

"I should be dead," she whispered to herself.

Vaguely, she recalled a talk with Debra.

Very odd. She had scarcely thought of her sister since the funeral.

Keri stood and stretched, actually hearing her limbs crack. It was as if her blood had frozen but something occurred during the time she was unconscious that thawed it out. Sucking in a deep breath of the frigid air, she paced back and forth in the confined space and tried to understand how she had regained her strength. Her mind was unusually clear, and she could recall every detail that had led up to her current situation: the guy in the alleyway; the cloth over her mouth; the ride in the blue car; his groping her butt. Her butt! He had given her a shot in the rear, not a drug that knocked her out but something else. Maybe the drug was the answer—maybe it protected her from the cold. She had simply imagined that she was dying.

"No," she said aloud as she stopped pacing. "I *was* dying."

A mystery, to be sure. But another thing puzzled her—she was not upset. She had been kidnapped, molested, left to die, but all these things were . . . well, just stuff that happened. Not that she was totally indifferent, but she wasn't crying. Lifting her hand, she brushed away the tears that had earlier frozen on her cheeks. She felt no need to save them. In fact, everything that had happened to her before tonight—her whole life for that matter— didn't seem important. She was alive now and she was locked in a grocery freezer. That was the present situation and that was all that mattered.

In the curious dark that did not totally obliterate her vision, Keri stared intently at the freezer door and thought again about how strong she felt. Strong enough, she dared to imagine, that she did not need to be rescued. Bouncing up and down in place, she marveled at how light she felt. Yet the sensation of supernatural power did not bring her joy or relief. Her emotional life felt as cool as the surrounding atmosphere.

Without thinking about it, Keri leapt toward the door and kicked it hard with her right foot. The wooden door frame shuddered. Feeling a rush of power, she took a few steps back and again leapt and kicked. The door bent; the metal hinges squealed. Two more violent kicks and the door exploded outward and fell to the floor. Yellow light from the grocery store poured into the freezer. Fog covered her like a magical shroud as she stepped from her icy prison.

"Shit," she muttered as she stared at what was left of the door. Even a karate master, with a closet full of black belts, she realized, could not have done what she just did. What was going on?

The grocery store was empty, the lights down low. Walking out of the back and into the aisles she was gripped by an intense hunger. She was close to the bakery goods and stopped and grabbed a box of chocolate doughnuts and gobbled them down— all eight of them. Not far away was a display of two-liter plastic Coke bottles, and she drank one of those as well. Still—it was incredible—she was hungry. Lucky her, to be locked in a grocery store at a time like this. She hurried to the deli section and found two lemon-herb roasting chickens, which she washed down with a carton of milk and a large bag of potato chips. She couldn't understand why she wasn't getting sick.

"Where is all this food going?" she asked aloud.

After the second chicken she felt sated and decided to make her way home. By now she was beginning to accept her phenomenal strength—she was in an extraordinarily accepting mood. The front doors were locked, but she broke out with a slight twist of her wrists. She didn't worry about the damage she left behind. The guy who had kidnapped her could pay for it.

Outside, she took a moment to get her bearings. She didn't recognize the street names but walking a block from the grocery store she came to the intersection of Main Street and Fourth—which was familiar. She was in Santa Ana, a bad section of the city where the wild elements of Orange County came to buy drugs and pick up hookers—so she had heard. Certainly the surrounding buildings were run-down—not a single one with a decent coat of paint.

Wait a second! What was wrong? The buildings were not the only objects relegated to black and white—she could find color nowhere, on the few trees that staggered up from the broken sidewalks, the scraggly bushes brushing against the boarded-up homes. It was as if the cold had damaged her eyes and left her color-blind. Yet, at the same time, her eyesight was sharper than ever. She could read the street signs on the next block, and the block beyond that. In fact, when she focused, her eyes seemed to telescope—she could read street signs a mile away. The silver radiance remained, faint but clear, circling over and around each object.

Yet she was color-blind. Like Oscar.

She walked swiftly toward the intersection. Before she could reach it, however, she became aware of a group of six tough-looking white boys hanging out in an alleyway on her side of the street. They were smoking and drinking and from their less than subtle mutters it was clear they had seen her. Trying to appear casual, she moved to the other side of the street. Bad strategy—she just told them she was scared. Yet in reality she was not fearful. Even when they threw down their smokes and bottles and jogged in her direction she didn't feel her heart pound. Their approach was an event, nothing more, the night was filled with them. Plus with her new-found strength, she could easily defend herself.

The leader was tall and skinny, thin light mustache, dirt on the upper lip, cold gray eyes—if that was their real color, she couldn't be sure. He wore a denim jacket and dark pants and moved with a twitch. Twenty at the most, his natural arrogance was fortified with man-made stimulants. His dilated pupils took her in from head to toe and he grinned with satisfaction.

"Who the hell are you?" he asked.

She stopped six paces from them. They fanned

out, a half circle of menace. None was over twenty, but each had been born on a mean street. Keri searched up and down the block and decided she was alone. Still, her calm remained.

"I don't want any trouble," she said quietly.

He laughed and glanced at his buddies. "Did you hear that? She thinks we're trouble." Then to her, "Hey, you come into our neighborhood and accuse us? What kind of rich bitch are you?"

Slowly she shifted her weight. Her control of each muscle in her feet and legs was extraordinary. She felt that if she were to kick at his face, she could brush a single eyelash a millimeter to the right or left. Of course she suspected she could also break his face in half. To the gang's surprise she took a step forward.

"I am not a bitch," she said firmly. "I am not rich. I am simply on my way home and I don't want any problems."

The leader came close and glared down at her, his beer breath on her face.

"You're the problem here," he said. "You don't belong here. But maybe you be nice to me and my pals and we let you go home. Get my meaning?"

She shook her head. "I will hurt you if you touch me."

He wiped the back of his arm across his mouth and put a hand on her shoulder. "Now how are you going to hurt me, little girl?" he asked.

She held his eye. "There are many ways I can. Take your hand off me."

He snorted and shook his head. He looked to his

buddies for confirmation of the fact that she must be crazy to talk to him that way. They smiled and nodded, enjoying the play. His gaze came back to her, a snap of his head, and he slowly moved his hand onto her left breast. He pawed it roughly and waited for her reaction, but she didn't give him one.

"You know, you feel good," he said finally.

She allowed a slight smile. "You don't feel so good."

He feigned insult. "Hey, babe, you haven't felt me."

"No. I mean you won't feel good."

"We'll see about that, girl."

He was lewd, he grabbed her hand and guided it toward his crotch. She got there before him, with her knee. She brought it up so suddenly, so hard, that everyone present heard the sound. The noise was soft and brittle, bone and tissue alike exploding. The guy bent only slightly with the impact but his expression disintegrated. He looked down at his groin and horror spread across his face as did the dark stain in his pants. Even Keri was stunned when he dropped to the ground and blood began to puddle around his midsection. She had not meant to hurt him that badly.

Hurt? He was bleeding so fast his internal organs must have ruptured. He would be dead in minutes, already she could see he was going into shock. One of his buddies knelt by his side and touched his hand.

"Stu?" he whispered.

Stu could not reply. He continued to hold his

crotch, but he could not patch the dam that had burst. Dark fluid soaked through his fingers. She assumed it was red; her color-blindness would not lift even for blood.

Out the corner of her eye, on her far right, she saw a short squat guy reach for something in his coat. Her body reacted instinctively, too fast for the boys to follow. In a blink his pistol was in her hand and the barrel of the gun was pointed at the side of his head. Using him as a shield, his arms twisted behind his back by her fearsome grip, she backed away from the gang.

"Like I said," she told them as the squat guy trembled in her arms. "I don't want any problems. But you come after me to avenge your friend, and you'll all die. OK?"

On the ground Stu gave a strangled gasp and lay still, his eyes open and locked in ghastly finality. The puddle of blood continued to spread, but his heart wasn't in it. The gang members backed off and nodded nervously.

"No problem," one of them said. "Just you stay away from here."

"What about me?" the guy in her arms cried to his buddies.

She whispered in his ear. "You, I will have for dinner. Don't struggle."

The guy whimpered as she yanked him down the street and around a corner. There she shoved him against a wall and stepped back and threw his gun two hundred yards down the street. She could only see in black and white, but it was enough to see he was the color of a bed sheet. He cowered as she glared at him.

"Now I will only let you live if you promise me to behave yourself for the rest of your life," she swore. "No more raping young women out for late strolls and no more hanging out with jerks like those guys. You go back to school and study to be a doctor."

He nodded anxiously. "OK. I promise." He hesitated. "Who are you?"

"I'm your guardian angel." She wagged a finger at him. "Remember your promise, I'll be back to check on you."

The guy fled. Keri laughed and started down the street, in the direction of Newport. But she had hardly walked twenty feet when she began to tremble. Her body had changed, her mind had altered, but deep inside she remained untouched and now that part began to wail.

She had just killed a guy!

She had dropped him bleeding to the ground. Plus she had almost been killed. What was she doing? A better question—*who* was she? She looked like Keri Weir and had all her memories, but she had to wonder if she hadn't died inside the freezer and been possessed by an evil spirit. That guy, Stu, might have been playing with her, but now he was a corpse on the asphalt.

"God," she whispered out loud. "What if he had family?"

Keri wanted to cry, but her new metabolism refused to produce tears. She didn't know whom she could talk to about what had happened to her. She wasn't sure if the change was permanent. All she knew was that it was no dream and that she was . . . hungry! She had to eat again, and now. Up ahead was a 7-Eleven, filled with doughnuts and candy bars and chips and milk. She had no money and was afraid to enter the store because she knew she would take what she wanted—she wouldn't be able to stop herself. Then maybe more people would get hurt. No, she had to get home.

Keri crossed the path of a bus a few minutes later and the driver let her climb aboard without the required fare. Perhaps he took pity on her, or maybe she frightened him with the wild expression in her eyes. The bus was heading toward Newport. She lay her head back against the seat and tried to come up with a rational explanation for what was happening to her. The only clue was the injection from her kidnapper. But had it been a shot? She had been delirious with his stun drug and with terror. The truth was that there probably was no reasonable explanation for what had become of her.

Maybe all this had something to do with aliens.

The bus took her to within two miles of her home, but as she climbed off the bus she decided to go see Oscar instead. The poor guy, he might still be waiting for her. The fact that his place was twice as far as her own did not intimidate her, and she didn't even consider stopping to get her car. She had been hiking for only a few minutes when she started to jog, and then to run. The sensation of movement was startling. She didn't know track records but realized she must be moving faster than any Olympic track star. The sidewalk flew beneath her feet. She was glad the roads were mostly deserted because if a cop had seen her, he would have flipped on his flashing lights and chased her. She thought again of Stu but it was a fleeting thought—her grief and horror refused to stay with her.

She reached Oscar's condo complex in less than ten minutes. Hardly panting, she rounded the parking lot and headed for the wooden deck that ran beside the water and his rear balcony. There she froze in midstride, below his wide windows, her hyper-alert mind shifting gears into a higher level of focus. The guy who had attacked her in the alley had been waiting for her. He had known when she was leaving and he had known her car. Before she blacked out she had caught a glimpse of his own car—saw that it was blue. Following Oscar home the previous night, she had noticed he had a blue car. Lots of people did.

But only Oscar had known she was going out then.

"You should have listened to your heart."

Who had said that? She could not remember.

"You knew the guy was not normal."

But it was true, Oscar had been far from normal. He needed to eat a lot, he was strong.

He was just like she was now.

"It was him," she said to herself. "He kidnapped me. He left me to die."

She hadn't died, though, and perhaps he intended for her to live. But how could she run to him when he had subjected her to such an ordeal? He was the last person she could trust. He was sick, and she had to go to the police and explain what he had done to her.

That would go over well. They'd ask why she hadn't died and how she had destroyed the freezer door. Plus, let us not forget, they would inquire about dead Stu around the block from the store. A few of the local boys, Keri, said they saw a girl who fit your description. Strong bitch, they said, bust his balls good. Right, bright idea, she should run to the police and lock herself in a cell while she was at it.

Keri ran from the condo complex. Again she broke records and didn't stop until she was standing at her front door. Struggling with Oscar earlier, she had lost her bag and the keys inside it, but she did not need them to break through her mother's locks. By now there was light in the east and she wondered if she would melt in the sun. She sort of hoped she would.

She didn't think she could live like this.

Yet a large part of her was unconcerned. More stuff.

She would breathe fire next and it wouldn't matter.

Inside, she went to the kitchen and ate three bananas and half a loaf of bread and what was left of her Friday night pizza. Her lower abdomen continued to feel crampy—freezing to death had not eliminated the condition. Sitting in her bedroom, she called the hospital. Her mother was asleep, and the nurse on duty would not wake her. Next she dialed

Clay, not sure what she would tell him. He answered in a drowsy voice but woke up when he heard who it was. Maybe he thought she was having second thoughts about the break-up.

"Having trouble sleeping?" he asked.

"Yeah." She paused. "Clay, you were right. That guy I met . . . he's no good. I have to stay away from him."

"Did you see him tonight?"

"I don't know."

"Keri?"

"Yeah, I saw him. It was bad. I won't see him again."

"What did he do? Did he hurt you?"

"He . . . it's complicated. He didn't hurt me. But I know he's dangerous. I wanted to tell you, but I'm all right." She stopped. "I don't know why I called."

"You sound scared."

She closed her eyes. "Yeah. It's scary."

"I'll come over, you shouldn't be alone at a time like this."

"No. It's not a good time. I need to sleep. I've been up all night."

He was hurt. "What have you been doing?"

"It's a long story, but I wasn't with him."

"You're confusing me, Keri."

"I'm pretty confused myself. Go back to sleep, Clay. I'll call you later, I promise."

He protested but she felt she had said enough. Finally she was able to lie back on her mat and pull her blankets tight. Only she couldn't sleep and it wasn't merely because of her fear Oscar would come to her apartment. Deep inside she sensed that sleep was unnatural to the transformation her body had undergone. She could close her eyes, she could rest, but she would never know true unconsciousness. Never again would she dream, either in color or in black and white. The truth of that bizarre fact came to her with unmistakable clarity. There was no escape from what she had become.

8

It was hunger that pulled her out of bed at ten in the morning. There was no food in the house. After taking sixty bucks from a shoe box she kept in her closet, she walked to the grocery store on the corner and bought four pounds of hamburger, two bags of buns, a head of lettuce, a pound of tomatoes, two onions, a pound of cheese, steak sauce, four bags of Oreos, four gallons of milk, three pounds of butter, and eight loaves of bread. She ate two bags of cookies on the walk home and drank half a gallon of milk. Once inside the apartment she cooked four cheeseburgers and ate them one after another, finishing the remainder of the gallon of milk. Only then did the empty ache in her stomach disappear.

"At least I'm not craving blood," she muttered

as she cleaned up. She worried about her finances. The way she figured it, she would need at least two hundred dollars a day just to stave off starvation. She was afraid to wander too far from home in case she got hungry. At the same time she knew she couldn't just sit in the apartment and wait for Oscar to show. For all she knew he might kill her for real this time.

Her abdomen continued to ache, and it felt hard and slightly swollen to the touch. Four Tylenols did nothing to dull the pain, and she suspected she could swallow the whole bottle and it wouldn't do a thing. She hoped she didn't have an alien growing inside her because she hated the mess they made when they burst out of people's guts.

Keri decided to visit her mom at the hospital. She took her car—her bag was lying on the ground under the driver's side. The world shone at her in glorious black and white, incredible clarity. Walking into her mother's room, she was mildly pleased to see her sitting up in bed and reading a trashy courtroom thriller. Her mom looked positively radiant. Maybe she'd had a near-death experience and seen the light. Yet her mother frowned when Keri sat on her bed.

"What happened to you?" her mother asked.

Keri shrugged. "What do you mean?"

Her mother studied her. "You look like you're the one who overdosed. You're pale, and your face . . . you look like you've lost weight."

"I haven't been dieting," Keri muttered.

"Your eyes look different, too."

"How?"

Her mother was puzzled. "I'm not sure. Oh, and your breath—it smells funny."

She hadn't noticed, but wished she had some . . . peppermints to hide the odor. "Thanks," Keri muttered.

"What did you do last night?" her mother asked.

"Nothing."

"Did you get laid?"

"No." She paused. "I didn't even see Oscar."

"He's the new guy?"

"No. He's history, I don't want to talk about him or myself. How are you feeling?"

"Wonderful." Her mother was thoughtful. "I had a dream last night."

"About Debra?" Keri blurted out.

Her mother was stunned. "You haven't said her name in two years. Why did you bring her up now?"

Keri ignored the question. "Was the dream about her?"

"Yes." Her mother took her hand. "Can I talk about it?"

"Sure."

Her mother shook her head. "What's happened to you? Usually when I say her name you run from the room."

"I can talk about her now, it's fine. I'm sorry I couldn't before. I'm sorry I forced you to suffer alone, after Dad left." Keri squeezed her hand. "Tell me about your dream."

"It was mostly uneventful, but the feeling that

permeated it was beautiful. The three of us were talking in her old room about a trip she was going on. We were both helping her pack. I remember how excited she was to be on her way."

"How did it end?"

"I don't remember."

"Did she give me any advice before it ended?"

"I don't know, it was only a dream. Why do you ask that?"

Keri shrugged and stood. "When are you getting out of here?"

"I have to talk to the doctor at noon, but then I'm free to go."

"Will you need a ride home? There's something I have to do right now."

"No. I think I can get home OK. I can always take the bus." Her mother hesitated. "What do you have to do?"

She stepped toward the door. "It doesn't matter. I'll talk to you later."

"Keri?"

Keri paused at the door. "Yes?"

"What's wrong with you?"

"Nothing."

"You're acting odd."

"It's just a mood." Then a foreboding swept over her. She might never see her mother again. "Take care of yourself, Mom. Stay away from the drugs. In the end they'll just kill you—and that's no fun."

Her mother stared. From nowhere a tear rolled over her cheek.

"I promise. You take care of yourself, Keri."

"I promise," Keri said.

She left the room. She left the hospital.

The face in the paper, the missing young man that the police thought was probably dead—she remembered now the thought she had when she'd blacked out in the freezer. The caption had said his name was Ted Lovett. He'd told her his name was Oscar.

Oscar what?

Her brain clicked on with crystal clarity. Ted Lovett had lived in Santa Monica with his parents. As he was an only child, they must still miss him terribly. They should be happy to talk to her, to hear he was alive.

She lucked out; the Lovetts were in the phone book. Unfortunately, when she knocked on their door at noon there was no answer. She decided to hang out near there until they returned. Go for a stroll on the beach, maybe take in a movie, eat. Of course she had to eat. She had only thirty bucks with her, so she found an all-you-can-eat buffet, practically bankrupted the place with her sixth and seventh helpings. The guy who worked behind the counter stared at her with wonder. He wanted to go out with her. She remembered reading that women who ate a lot and remained thin were sexy to guys. She laughed at his invitation, told him she was pregnant.

"You were just so lonely and horny you had to go ahead and sleep with him."

Who had said that? Another true remark.

Keri returned to the Lovetts' house at six in the evening. She chewed on some peppermints that she had bought. The door was opened by a sixty-year-old woman with thinning gray hair and a round sad face. Her eyes reminded Keri of Oscar's, their depth and shape, perhaps their color—although Keri couldn't be sure of the latter. Keri couldn't hear anyone else in the house, and her hearing was damn fine. Sitting through two movies in Westwood, she'd had to stuff tissues in her ears to keep from getting a headache. All her senses were incredibly sharp. The woman was baking shortbread cookies: butter, flour, sugar, pecans, a dash of vanilla. The smell made Keri hungry all over again.

"May I help you?" the woman asked.

"Are you Mrs. Lovett?"

"Yes."

Keri hesitated. The woman could be a grandmother.

"Are you the mother of Ted Lovett?" she asked carefully.

The woman's lower lip trembled. "Yes. Who are you?"

"My name is Keri Weir. I saw an article a year ago in the paper about your son. He disappeared suddenly one evening?"

She was guarded. "Did you know Ted?"

"Mrs. Lovett, I don't know how to say this, but I may have been with your son two days ago. But before you get your hopes up, I need to see his picture again. All I have is a memory of the snapshot in the paper from last year."

The poor woman stopped and took a deep breath. She stepped aside.

"Please come in," she said hastily. "I have a picture of Ted in the other room. I'll get it for you." She hurried away. "Where do you think you saw Ted?"

Keri called after her. "Please, Mrs. Lovett, let me see his picture before I say any more. I hate coming here like this because I know it must be a torture for you."

The woman reappeared a minute later, her eyes damp. She held her son's picture to her chest like a shield over her broken heart. Keri gently took it from her hands and studied it in the dim light of the living room. Yet the lack of light was not an obstacle for Keri—she would have recognized the face in a perfectly black room. The young man in the photo was heavier than Oscar, his gaze less penetrating, his hands less elegant. Yet it was the same guy, Oscar was Ted Lovett—come back from the abyss.

"Is it him?" the woman asked tightly.

Keri sighed and nodded. "Yes."

"Oh God." The woman staggered and Keri shot out a supporting arm. "Are you sure?"

"I'm positive, Mrs. Lovett. Your son lives in Balboa Beach. He goes by the name of Oscar. He has a condo there, and he supports himself as an artist."

The woman frowned. "But Ted was never an artist. You must be mistaken."

"I'm not mistaken. He's an artist now, a very good one, but he's changed in many ways since you last saw him."

The woman was having trouble keeping up. "How has he changed?"

"Please, let's sit down. I have questions I have to ask you as well." She took the woman's arm and led her to the couch. Keri held her hand as she spoke. "Before Ted disappeared, did he speak of a young woman?"

Mrs. Lovett's face darkened. "Yes. He had met a girl that he became obsessed with. I told the police about her. She was a bad seed, I knew it from the start."

"How did you know? How did she behave?"

"I never met her, and that was a problem. She wouldn't let Ted bring her here. Worse, she never let Ted know where she lived. He had to wait for her to call." She wiped her eyes. "She called the night he vanished and told him to meet her at a restaurant on Montana Avenue. The police think she was part of a gang of kidnappers or a member of a cult."

"What was her name?"

"Dara Smith, or at least that's what she said. I'm sure it was a lie."

"Did the police ever locate her?"

"No, we had no way to find her. Not even a description." With something close to desperation, she asked Keri, "Is Ted with this girl now?"

"I don't know. But he spoke of a young woman who led him through a huge change a year before."

"What is this change you keep saying?"

"I don't know how to explain it."

The woman trembled. "Please, if you have seen my son, you must take me to him."

"I'd rather bring him to you, if he'll come."

"But why?"

Keri patted her hand. "I hate doing this to you. I know when I leave here that you're going to doubt everything I've told you. But the truth is your son is alive. It's also true that he hasn't contacted you in over a year—of his own free will."

The woman showed bitterness. "If he is alive, then how do you know he's free to do what he wants?"

It was an excellent question, one Keri hadn't considered. It was possible this Dara remained in the background and manipulated him. It was also possible that Oscar had nothing whatsoever to do with her abduction the previous night, although she doubted that. The coincidences were simply too blatant.

"What kind of car did Ted drive?" Keri asked.

"A Honda."

"What color was it?"

"White. Why?"

"It's nothing." Keri stood up suddenly. "I will talk to Os . . . to Ted. I have to see him anyway about something else, and I'll tell him that he should contact you immediately."

Mrs. Lovett stood and grabbed her arm. "Please, if you're going to see him take me with you. If there's even a possibility that it's Ted, I have to go with you."

"I'm sorry, I can't do that."

She was desperate. "But why?"

"It might be dangerous."

"How? My son wouldn't hurt me."

Keri shook her head. "This must all sound insane to you. Honestly, I'll do what I can to have him contact you." She moved to the door. "In either case, I'll call you tomorrow."

Keri got out of the house before having to answer any more questions. She left the woman crying and felt bad about that. At the same time she didn't feel nearly the guilt she would have experienced before her episode in the freezer. She continued to wonder what kind of shot could have altered her very character. Also, she had made a significant decision while with the woman. The previous night she had assumed Oscar must be avoided at all costs, but now she was going to go see him. What choice did she have? Who else could explain what had happened to her? He was dangerous—but so was she.

"Just ask Stu," she said as she got back in her car.

She stopped at a McDonald's before driving back to Orange County: three Big Macs, four large fries, six shakes, a couple of Danish—she used up the last of her money. Her abdomen continued to swell, although the cramps had eased up some. The alien was on his way. Seventeen and pregnant—whatever—just more stuff to bounce off her super-cool attitude. If he ate her after she gave birth to him it would be a drag but she couldn't cry about it.

She drove toward Oscar's place.

She knew he'd be waiting for her.

9

He answered the door when she knocked; he looked good in black and white. Seen through her magically sharp vision, his clothes were various shades of gray: a loose-hanging sports coat, nice shirt, tight pants. He stepped aside and let her in—without comment—but she thought she detected a flash of warmth in the depths of his eyes. She realized then that his vision was deeper than her own, that whatever change she had undergone, he had gone farther with it.

They were not alone. A man stood near the balcony, facing the relatively silent harbor. When he turned, she saw he was fifty and looked like a modern-day prophet, a dark beard below gentle eyes, etched with lines of sorrow and matured by understanding. He nodded, almost apologetically, and Keri immediately understood that he knew what she had gone through in the freezer. She could see he had gone through a similar trauma. All three of them were changed.

"OK," she said. "I'm here. What's going on?"

Oscar gestured for her to have a seat. "We're happy you made it, and we plan to answer as many of your questions as we can." He sat across from her on the couch. The man moved toward the couch but remained standing for the moment. He was tall and well-built, yet his cheeks, like Oscar's, were hollow—the aesthetic artist, perhaps the enigmatic genius. The intelligence on the man's face was obvious. Oscar added, "But before we begin, may we ask where you were all day?"

"Didn't you have me followed?"

"You're not easy to follow," the man said. "By the way, my name is Gary Schelling."

"Pleased to meet you, Mr. Schelling—I think. You know who I am." She glanced at Oscar. "But who are you?"

He shrugged. "Call me Oscar. One name is as good as another."

"That depends, doesn't it?" she said.

"Where did you go today?" Oscar repeated.

"When did you lose me?" she asked.

"After you left your mother at the hospital," Oscar said. "You were driving like a maniac."

She shook her head. "You talk, and then I'll decide what I want to tell you."

Gary Schelling nodded and finally sat on the couch beside Oscar.

"That sounds fair to me," he said. "And since it's my fault we're all in this condition, perhaps I should be the first to explain. But before I do, may I ask, Keri, if you recognize my face?"

She studied him. "No, are you someone famous?"

"In certain circles. My full name is *Dr.* Gary Schelling. Until two years ago I was considered by many to be the best geneticist in the world."

"What happened two years ago?" she asked.

Without hesitating, he said, "I began to experiment on myself."

She nodded slowly. "The injection I got before I was dumped in the freezer."

Oscar was surprised. "You weren't supposed to know about that."

"Why not?" she asked.

Dr. Schelling raised a hand to interrupt them. "You'll have many questions. Let me explain for a few minutes before you ask them. A lot will become clear."

Keri relaxed deeper into her chair. "I hope so."

"You may be aware that for the last ten years various scientific groups around the world have been mapping the gene sequence of human DNA. The results of these discoveries often appear in the papers or on TV. You've probably seen articles announcing that the cause of such and such a disease has been found. It is hoped that in the future, we will be able to correct any flaws in our genes before disease manifests." He paused. "Is any of this familiar to you?"

"I read the newspapers, Dr. Schelling," Keri said.

"Very good," he continued. "But what you probably never read in the papers is that there are large sections of our DNA that have no genes attached. To most scientists these are considered 'dead' areas. Usually they are of no interest to people in the field—there is nothing there, so the thinking goes, so there is no reason to examine barren strands. Yet, for reasons I have not been able to explain even to myself, I have been drawn to these blank areas. Often I'd ask myself the questions: 'Why did nature not condense the genes if these areas were not important?' 'Why have them at all?' These are fundamental questions, and, I thought, very reasonable ones. Because the products of evolution, in my opinion, are extremely logical and seldom wasteful.

"I began to study the empty strands in earnest. This brought amusement and even concern from my colleagues. They saw me as studying nothing. Even under the most powerful electron microscopes, there wasn't much to see. The unattached strands appeared to be there for support, nothing else. Yet I couldn't leave them alone, and still, I didn't know why.

"Five years ago I was studying a sample of human DNA that had come from a member of my staff. His name was Dr. Wheeler and he was in his late seventies and suffering from a serious heart condition. I had a sample of his skin cells under my microscope and was in the process of staining them for an elaborate sequencing procedure when I heard that Dr. Wheeler was not feeling well and was going home for the day. I muttered my approval and continued to prepare my sample. Perhaps ten minutes went by when I noticed a most mysterious phenomena, one I had never seen before. Under my electron microscope, I saw several of the empty strands of the DNA rotate ninety degrees counterclockwise. It was as if they were being turned by a miniature motor—I could hardly believe my eyes. Moments later an assistant burst into my lab and exclaimed that Dr. Wheeler had just had a heart attack and died. Naturally I forgot all about my sample because Dr. Wheeler was a good friend and had worked with me for many years. But a week later, after his funeral, the image of the rotating strands came back to haunt me. I wondered if my subconscious had driven me to this discovery. If the chance use of a dying man's skin sample had not in reality been more than chance."

"I'm sorry," Keri interrupted. "I don't exactly understand what your discovery was."

"I wasn't sure myself, not at first," Dr. Schelling said. "But I had an idea and it fascinated and terrified me at the same time. I asked myself: 'What if the rotation of the barren strands of DNA was a kind of fundamental death response?' Let me explain. Most doctors would define death as the cessation of breathing, the stopping of the heart. But we all know that with modern resuscitation techniques people who have had their heartbeats and breathing cease for as long as five minutes have been brought back to life. There have been examples, when extreme cold is involved, where the time has been lengthened to as much as twenty minutes. This is because cold slows down the destruction of brain cells. It is the brain that is most sensitive to the need for oxygen. It is the brain that dies first, and a flat EEG has become the benchmark for the definition of death. In some states it has become a law that an EEG be performed before a death certificate can be signed.

"But what about the ninety-degree rotation of the barren strands of DNA at the moment of death? It seemed to me this was a much more primal definition of death. I began to investigate to see if it was a constant at each death. I took samples of mice cells and placed them under the electron microscope, and then killed the animals. And in each case, at the moment of their deaths, the strands rotated. I was beside myself with amazement. The phenomena was so obvious, so prevalent, yet no one had thought to look for it."

"Excuse me," Keri interrupted again. "From what you're saying, these samples of cells were no longer attached to their donors when the donors died. How could the DNA rotate? I mean, how did the sample know what was happening to the donor?"

Dr. Schelling nodded. "That is an excellent question. It may be the most important question of our time, and I'm sorry to say it is still a question I can't answer. To solve the mystery one is almost required to postulate the existence of a soul. For something must connect the sample cells to the donor. At least at the moment of death there must be a connection."

"Did you check cells that were still attached to the mice when they died?" Keri asked.

"Yes. The results were the same—it made no difference."

"Fascinating," Keri remarked. "Did you publish your findings?"

"No. I kept them secret."

"Why?" Keri asked.

"Because I wanted to see if I could block the rotation."

"You just lost me," Keri said, although he had not lost her at all.

"I asked myself another question," Dr. Schelling replied. " 'What if the rotation of the empty strands superseded every other *symptom* of death?' In other words, if the rotation was prevented, would death be prevented? To be frank I didn't think it possible. If the brain cells died, I reasoned, then the person would still die. I doubted death could be so easily cheated. Yet, what the hell, I thought, I had to give it a try."

Keri frowned. "How?"

"It wasn't easy. I had to genetically design a compound that would fit into the empty strands in question—like a piece in a jigsaw puzzle—and stop them from turning. It took me two years to develop the correct formula, and then another year to figure out how to deliver it into the system. But in the end I was able to inject a mouse with what I called Lazarus9, kill the mouse, and then watch him return to life."

"Shit," Keri muttered, realizing the very personal

implications of what he was saying. "How did you kill the mice?"

"Usually by smothering them," Dr. Schelling said. "You want to ask another question but you're afraid. I understand your hesitation. What if I decapitated a mouse? Would it still return to life?"

Keri nodded slowly. "Would it?"

Dr. Schelling paused. "Yes."

"It would walk around without a head?"

"For a few minutes. Then it would quickly grow a new one."

"Oh God," Keri whispered. "That's impossible."

"I thought it impossible, too, and yet it happened. What had I discovered? God's secret code? I worked in my lab in total privacy late at night. I didn't know how I could possibly share my discovery with the world. I worried that it could be the end of the human race. Yet I also wondered if it could be humanity's salvation."

Keri nodded. "If no one ever died—if no one could die—what would they do? How would they behave?"

"Exactly. Immortality would require an incredible maturity that we weren't ready for. At the same time I couldn't simply bury my research. I noticed that my mice did not simply return to life. . . ."

"They returned changed," Keri said.

"Yes. It wasn't long before I saw that they returned stronger and more alert. They also required much more food because their metabolisms were working at a much higher rate. These mice were 'born again' and were living at their full potential.

Yet ironically they had achieved this only by dying."

Oscar spoke. "It makes you wonder if religious leaders of the past didn't understand this phenomena when they spoke of the need for the death of the flesh before the spirit could be reborn."

Keri nodded. "It makes me wonder if the authors of vampire stories didn't know what they were talking about."

Dr. Schelling agreed. "It's possible that the rotation of the empty DNA strand has in the past been stopped by cruder methods. Perhaps the origins of voodoo and zombies came from an accidental discovery of herbs that replicate Lazarus9."

"Why Lazarus9? Why not Lazarus1?" Keri asked.

Dr. Schelling shrugged. "The ninth variation of the formula worked. The first eight did not."

Keri looked at him closely. "You tried it on yourself."

"I had to."

She shook her head. "Don't give me that. You wanted to try it on yourself. You wanted to see how you would change. You wanted to live forever."

"You're right on both points. Still, I could not in good conscience give it to another human being, and a human trial was the only way I could further my research."

"You're hard on Dr. Schelling," Oscar said. "I'm surprised you don't acknowledge his courage."

Keri gestured. "I don't know what to acknowledge at this point. Tell me, Dr. Schelling, how you did it?"

"The Lazarus9 had to be taken while my heart was still beating. That way my blood could carry it to each of my cells. As to the means of my death . . . I overdosed myself on sleeping pills."

"Sounds easier than freezing to death," Keri muttered.

"There are much worse ways to die than pills or freezing," Oscar said quietly.

Dr. Schelling raised a hand. "Please hear the entire story, Keri, before deciding whether we are misguided or not."

"Please continue," Keri said. "How did you feel when you woke up from being dead?"

"Wonderful. You know the experience. All my physical and mental abilities were greatly enhanced. I was delighted with the change. But I was also relieved for a reason I have not explained to you. A private reason that had driven my research from the beginning."

"Dara," Oscar whispered.

Keri whirled. "The girl who changed you?"

Oscar nodded. "Yes."

"My daughter," Dr. Schelling said in a gentle voice. "She was suffering from a rare form of leukemia. The disease was in its last stages. There was no hope for her." He gestured helplessly. "I gave her a shot of Lazarus9."

"That's not all," Keri corrected. "The formula only works if you die after you take it. Am I right? You gave her a shot and then you killed her?"

Dr. Schelling hesitated. "True."

Keri sat up and sharpened her voice. "Did you tell her ahead of time?"

"Keri, the girl was dying," Oscar interjected.

"Did you tell her, Dr. Schelling?" Keri demanded.

The doctor was thoughtful. "How could I tell her?"

Keri sat back. "You could have told me."

The men stared at her. The burden of guilt was on their shoulders. Yet Keri felt shame over her outburst. She had not heard their entire story. She could only imagine what Dr. Schelling had gone through while watching his daughter approach death. Yet it was ironic that the cure, *his* cure, was to kill her.

"What we did to you was not easy," Oscar said.

Dr. Schelling nodded sadly. "What I did to my daughter was also very difficult. But when it was over, when she had changed, I had another problem. Her disease was gone, but she had been altered, her very personality, her essence if you like. Now, you have already experienced how a sense of detachment dominates after going through the death process. Before giving my daughter Lazarus9, I suspected she would end up with a more aloof attitude. Whether that was a blessing or a curse, I wasn't sure, but I simply felt I couldn't allow my daughter to die when I had the means to save her. But Dara became more than detached, she became outright scary."

"How so?" Keri asked.

"When I explained what I had done to her, she stole a beaker of Lazarus9 from my laboratory and injected it into her brother—my son, Eric—and killed him." Dr. Schelling shuddered. "I found out later she had strangled him to death."

"How was Eric after the change?" Keri asked.

Dr. Schelling shook his head. "Bad. Like her."

"Can you define bad?" Keri asked.

"They were cruel, devoid of all conscience," Dr. Schelling said. "They no longer had a sense of right or wrong, the very idea amused them."

"Did they still care for you, as their father?" Keri asked.

The doctor shrugged. "I don't know. Maybe."

"Dara is still sensitive, in certain ways," Oscar added.

Keri was surprised that she felt jealous. It was faint, and she was detached from it, but it was there nevertheless. "In what ways?" she asked.

Oscar shook his head. "It doesn't matter."

"Did you sleep with her?" Keri asked.

"It doesn't matter," Oscar repeated.

"How is Eric?" she asked.

"A walking nightmare, uncontrollable," Dr. Schelling said. "And he used to be such a sweet boy."

"How old were they when this happened?"

"Dara was twenty, Eric eighteen," Dr. Schelling said. "They haven't aged in the last two years. I doubt they ever will. None of us will."

"Why did they turn bad?" Keri asked. "Why didn't I?"

Oscar spoke. "We suspect that the manner in which a person dies has an effect on how he or she turns out, although this cannot be the whole reason. When Dara and Eric and the rest of their gang changed me, they buried me alive to the sound of Satanic chants. None of them is a Satanist, but they acted the part to increase my terror."

"Yet you managed to maintain your natural goodness?" Keri asked with a trace of sarcasm.

Oscar stared at her. "I am not who I was, Keri, but I am not a monster either."

"Nor are you," Dr. Schelling told her.

"I don't get this. I was thrown in a freezer to die—you guys did it, right?"

"Yes," Oscar admitted. "I did it."

"But you're implying that terror is the one thing that could have made me turn out bad. Let me tell you, guys, I was pretty scared. I'm surprised I don't need an exorcism right now. Or maybe I do—I don't know." She stopped. "Did you know I killed a guy last night?"

"Yes," Dr. Schelling said. "We saw."

"And you let me do it?" Keri asked, disgusted.

"We didn't know you were going to do it," Oscar said. "And it was necessary to leave you alone right after your transformation so that you could discover your abilities."

"No," Keri said. "You two left me alone so that you could observe me to see what I had turned into."

"That is true as well," Dr. Schelling admitted. "But Oscar is not lying to you."

"But what did you think when you saw me kill that guy?" Keri asked.

"We were worried," Oscar said. "But you were attacked. You were only protecting yourself. We noted that you did not harm the second guy, when you had the chance."

"And to answer your other question," Dr. Schelling said. "We had you abducted and killed in the manner we did because you *had* to know that you were going to die. We believe that having no knowledge of one's impending death makes the terror worse. Also, there was the element of the cold we subjected you to. To freeze to death is considered one of the easiest ways to go. At the same time, as I mentioned earlier, the cold protects the brain cells from dying so rapidly."

"What does that matter?" Keri asked. "You had mice grow fresh heads. Whatever brain cells died would have grown back."

"Yes," Dr. Schelling said. "But they probably wouldn't have been identical to the originals. We were trying to minimize the wild cards with you. Understand, we don't have all the answers. Although three dozen people have undergone the transformation, there is still much we don't know about it. Logically, I thought the cold might make a difference."

"None of your other three dozen victims died that way?" Keri asked.

"They were not my victims," Dr. Schelling said. "The ones I referred to—they were Dara's and Eric's."

"You are the first one Dr. Schelling has willingly given the formula to since he gave it to his daughter," Oscar explained.

Keri was astounded. "Did Dara and Eric force it on the others?"

"Yes," Dr. Schelling said, pain in his voice. "They stole a substantial amount of Lazarus9 from me before I could stop them, and with it they were able to create two dozen fiends."

"Two dozen? You just said three dozen," Keri said.

"They changed three dozen," Oscar explained. "They later destroyed twelve of those."

"Why?" Keri asked. "They turned out too nice?"

Dr. Schelling sighed again. "Essentially."

"How did they destroy them?"

"They incinerated them," Dr. Schelling said.

Keri grimaced. "Did they keep you prisoner?"

"Yes," he replied.

"How?"

"There were a lot of them and they were very strong."

She turned to Oscar. "Did they keep you prisoner as well?"

"No. I quickly understood what they were looking for in me. I convinced them that I was like them. Then I escaped with Dr. Schelling."

"They don't know where you are?" Keri asked.

"No," Dr. Schelling said. "But they search for us, for me in particular."

"They have run out of Lazarus9," Oscar explained. "They don't know how to make it and as a result they cannot expand their gang."

"Why do they want to expand?" Keri asked.

"I don't believe they want to expand indefinitely," Dr. Schelling said. "They do want to create an elite order, and I suspect their ultimate goal is to take over the world. I know that sounds absurd, but if they can build a group of ten thousand, they might be able to do it. They—we—are much stronger and smarter than normal people. Once they gain a foothold in politics or in the military, nothing could stop them."

"Have they changed people from all walks of life?" Keri asked.

"No, mainly teenagers," Dr. Schelling said. "Children have a tendency to go insane after the change. The shock is too great for their minds. With older people, the personality is too fixed. The individuals do not turn bad in the manner Dara and Eric prefer. At least that is my theory from observing their efforts."

"How exactly did you escape from the others?" Keri asked Oscar.

"I told you, I convinced Dara I was like her and Eric."

"Did you have to kill someone to do that?" Keri asked.

Oscar lowered his head. "There are things I was forced to do that I regret. I prefer not to talk about them."

"Was changing me one of those things?" Keri asked. When neither answered, she persisted,

"What did you want with me? How did you know I would not turn out bad? And please don't tell me that I had such a sweet smile and a nice aura that you thought I was and always would be an angel."

"Dara and Eric had nothing to do with your change," Dr. Schelling said. "They know nothing about it."

"We hope," Oscar added.

"You haven't answered my other questions," Keri said.

"We changed you because we needed you," Dr. Schelling said.

It was the last answer Keri expected. "What do you need with me?"

They glanced at each other uneasily.

"We need what you carry," Oscar said finally.

"What I carry?" Of course she knew what they meant.

"You're pregnant," Dr. Schelling said. "You must know this by now. Your metabolism is operating at such high speed that the gestation period for your child should be nine days instead of nine months."

Keri glared at Oscar. "You deliberately knocked me up, before you altered me."

"Yes," he said. "We had to."

"Why?" Keri demanded. "What kind of monster will this child be?"

"We cannot say exactly what it will be," Dr. Schelling replied. "But we do know it will be unique, a cross between what we are and what we were. A hybrid of life and death. It is this child who will stop the others. Nothing else can stop them."

"How do you know this?" Keri asked. "This child might be the first one to help them succeed."

"It's possible," Oscar said. "That the child will be beyond our control is a given, but we had to try something."

"This is insane," Keri protested. "It's a shot in the dark—this kid could turn out to be the antichrist."

"There's something else," Dr. Schelling said gravely. "Another key to the puzzle of Lazarus9. I am at heart a scientist, but now you must forgive me for I have to get metaphysical. Since each of us has changed—including Dara and Eric and their insane minions—we have all dreamed of a dark figure surrounded by a dazzling white light. Oscar dreamed of him even before he was given Lazarus9." He paused. "What is the matter, Keri?"

She shook her head. "Nothing."

"You have dreamed of him as well," Oscar said.

She hesitated. "Yes."

"Did you speak to him?" Dr. Schelling asked.

"Yes. Did you guys?"

"No. None of us has," Oscar said. "But we thought he might have spoken to you. What did he say?"

"He asked me if he should come. He kept asking me that again and again. I don't know what he meant."

"He was asking if you would give birth to him," Oscar said.

Keri sneered. "You don't know that."

"We know nothing for sure," Dr. Schelling agreed. "We're groping in the dark. But the physical effect of Lazarus9 has opened a nonphysical door. Perhaps it is a door that should never have been opened—we don't know—but it's too late to go back. We have all been dreaming of this black figure because he is on his way."

"You're saying his coming is destined?" Keri asked.

"It would appear destined now," Oscar said.

"How come you dream if none of you sleeps?" she asked.

"We still need to rest, and during that rest we *see* dreams," Dr. Schelling said.

"You must get a lot of work done," Keri remarked. "Oscar, how did you know you would get me pregnant the first time?"

"Our sense of smell is highly developed. I could tell you were ovulating."

"Get off it!" Keri said.

"Your senses will refine further with time," Dr. Schelling said. "Please believe what Oscar tells you. Also, his sperm is far more powerful than human sperm. It was inevitable, so to speak, that it would find what it was looking for."

"But I was alive and normal at the time," Keri muttered.

"The black figure wanted it that way," Oscar said.

"How do you know? You said he never spoke to either of you."

Dr. Schelling raised his hand. "This is where we enter a metaphysical realm and again I must apologize. Oscar bumped into you by chance, but when he did he knew he was supposed to meet you. That the dark figure had willed it. That is why we were fairly sure you would survive the change with your conscience intact. Since the change we all have experienced making decisions intuitively."

"Even Dara and Eric?" she asked.

"Even them," Dr. Schelling said. "They know things they shouldn't."

The comment had an ominous ring. Worse, there was something foreboding in it as well. Both Dr. Schelling and Oscar paused and appeared to listen deeply. Keri did likewise but couldn't hear anything beyond the normal sounds of the harbor: the lapping of the water, the faint churning of powerboat propellers; the laughter and talk of people out on their boats. Dr. Schelling and Oscar looked at each other, concerned.

"Where did you go today?" Oscar asked her.

"To see your parents," Keri said.

Dr. Schelling stood suddenly. "They had that house under observation."

Oscar also stood. "After all this time?"

"They are mad but patient," Dr. Schelling replied, moving toward the balcony. He stopped in midstride at a knock on the front door.

Keri stood. "Are you expecting anyone?"

"No one knows we're here," Oscar whispered.

The person knocked again. Louder.

10

What followed next was like a scene from a bad movie. Oscar and Dr. Schelling quickly moved to a closet. In the blink of an eye they were holding pump-action shotguns. Dr. Schelling stepped behind the door, Oscar reached to open it. He gestured for Keri to go into the other room, but she chose not to. Maybe it was a guy delivering pizza, she thought. She was hungry again, but perhaps she should have been more scared. Of course she hadn't seen Dara and Eric up close and personal. If she had known them, she would have run screaming from the condo.

"Who is it?" Oscar called out.

The voice sounded weak. "It's Clay Stanton."

"It's just Clay," Keri said and moved toward the door. "I told him you lived down here. Let me talk to him a moment."

Oscar stopped her at the door and whispered in her ear. "He's not alone, Keri."

She looked at him. "You sure?"

Oscar nodded. "Hear the fear in his voice."

Dr. Schelling pumped a shotgun shell in the chamber.

Keri nodded. Clay did not sound like himself.

"What do you want me to do?" she whispered.

"Get away from the door," Oscar said softly.

"I can't do that," she hissed. "If you both start shooting, Clay will get hurt. Besides, I didn't think these guys could be killed by bullets."

"They cannot be killed except with fire," Dr. Schelling said. "But if we blow out their brains, they'll be stopped for some time. Please, Keri, stand back."

"Keri!" Clay called from the other side of the door. "Open up."

"Please," Oscar said.

"No," she insisted. "I must warn him."

"They already have him," Oscar said gravely, but he nodded for her to open the door. Saying a brief prayer that Clay was alone, she turned the doorknob.

Clay was with a friend. She stood off to his left and slightly behind. She appeared to have a hold on Clay's left arm. Keri couldn't be sure though. The girl was blond and beautiful, with a large sensual mouth and cold green eyes. Yes, Keri could see color there, only there, in the center of this young woman's cold soul. Perspiration dampened

Clay's face, and he swallowed thickly before speaking.

"Hello, Keri," he said.

"What are you doing here?" she asked.

He sounded apologetic. "I came to see if you were OK. Couldn't find you at home. Couldn't find you down here, either, until I ran into this girl—and her friends."

The girl spoke, liquid ice. "Hello, Ted."

Oscar nodded. "Dara. So you still watch my parents' house."

"But you never go home," Dara replied.

"There's no going home for any of us," Oscar said.

Dara smiled faintly, the amusement of a ghost. Her skin was much paler than the rest of theirs, an apparition carved from an arctic nightmare. She shifted her right arm and Clay gasped—she definitely had his arm and was doing unpleasant things with it.

"Your place is with us," Dara said. "Come. Is Daddy around?"

Oscar cocked his shotgun but didn't point it at her. "You have to leave, Dara. Let go of Clay."

Dara tossed her hair. "It has taken us a long time to find you." She glanced behind the door. "Both of you, Daddy. We can't just leave, no, that wouldn't be fun."

Dr. Schelling stepped from behind the door and aimed his shotgun at her.

"You know I won't give you any Lazarus9," Dr.

Schelling said. "You can torture me all you want, it'll make no difference."

"Torture?" Dara said as she pulled Clay closer. "That is not my style. And as much as I would like to stand here and chat, we have to be on our way." She paused. "The others are waiting."

"Let go of my friend," Keri snapped.

Dara stared at her. "You are newborn, and you are pregnant. You are the one. You will come with us as well."

"Like I give a damn what you say, bitch," Keri replied.

Dara grinned and twisted Clay's arm harder. Clay cried out in pain, and Dara pressed her cheek close to his damp face. In that moment Keri's peculiar detachment wavered. Clay looked like a lost child, searching for his mom to save him.

"Oh, Clay," Keri moaned. "Please let him go."

"Not yet," Dara whispered.

"Why is she so strong?" he wept as Dara twisted his arm even more. Clay tried to bend over in pain, but she wouldn't let him. Obviously she wanted to use him as a shield. Her father showed no hesitation about shooting her and kept angling for an opening. Oscar, on the other hand, remained calm.

"You're right, this isn't your style," Oscar told Dara. "Let him go and we can discuss this. He's not one of us, he doesn't belong here."

"But he is available," Dara said. "I use what is available. Like I used you, Ted."

Dara gave a sharp yank. Clay choked and screamed.

"Keri!" he cried.

"Stop!" Keri shouted, stepping forward. Oscar grabbed her.

"She is stronger than any of us," Oscar said.

Clay continued to thrash in Dara's vicelike grip.

"Do something!" Keri yelled at Oscar.

"I have a suggestion," Dara said gently. "I will release your friend, unharmed, if you will put down your weapons and leave this condo and climb in a van we have waiting in the parking lot. You have to do this now; the noise we make will bring the police and none of us wants that." She paused. "Otherwise I will rip off Clay's left arm. You have five seconds to decide. One . . ."

"Dara," Oscar said. "This is not necessary."

"Two . . ."

"There will be no more Lazarus9," Dr. Schelling said flatly.

"Three . . ."

"She's hurting me!" Clay cried.

"Four . . ."

"Goddamn you witch!" Keri swore, pushing Oscar aside as he tried to stop her. Oscar knew Dara only too well, knew her strength, her heart—how her beautiful face hid the insect that crawled inside her skull. Even though Dara was encumbered with Clay, she was able to deflect Keri's charge effortlessly, sending Keri falling back on her butt. Simultaneously Dara shifted Clay so he was directly in front of her. For a moment, as Keri landed on the carpeted floor, time was suspended.

But the green in Dara's eyes faded to deep black as she completed the sequence.

"Five," Dara said. It appeared a joke, a relief, Clay stopped struggling and stood upright suddenly. A peculiar calm filled his expression. But then Dara's smile widened and she showed them her prize, taking it from behind Clay's back—an arm, yanked clean from its socket. Blood spurted out of Clay's shoulder and he staggered to the side of the door. Dara let him go, she didn't appear to be worried about her father's shotgun aimed at her head.

"Kill me, Daddy," she said, blood on her face, the arm still in her hand. "I know I'm not the little girl you always wanted."

Dr. Schelling did not fire. The horror was too much for him. The scientist reached out to support Clay, but the poor guy was already on his way to the floor, to where Keri lay. Dr. Schelling muttered something about God and how sorry he was, but neither of them could help Clay as he rolled onto his back and began to convulse. In the black and white world of the deathless zombies, the blood spread like a pool of ink that had been set aside for entries in Satan's diary. Clay wanted to speak but ended up gagging. Keri placed her hand over the wound, but there was no stopping the blood.

Plus, the fun had just begun.

The glass door to the balcony exploded in a thousand shards as four black-clad figures leapt into the living room: two guys, two girls, each armed with semiautomatics. Oscar fired at Dara, but she was no longer where she had been standing. Unfazed, he whirled and fired two shots at the new intruders, hitting both the girls in the face. White skin splattered into dark brain tissue and the females went down. But their partners returned fire and Oscar staggered back against the wall, bleeding from his stomach.

Dr. Schelling was on his knees and firing. He took down one of the guys, but the other hit him hard in the shoulder and he fell back. Near where Keri knelt beside Clay was a white stand that held a small glass globe. Keri grabbed it and threw it hard at the guy's head. To her relief and surprise it stunned him; he dropped to one knee. Keri took the opportunity to seize Dr. Schelling's shotgun. Still on her knees, she shot the guy in the face as he climbed back to his feet. His brains splattered the balcony behind him.

And this guy was supposed to come back to life?

Clay stopped gagging and grabbed Keri's hand. He struggled for breath, but his face was strangely calm. It was clear he was near death.

"Keri," he gasped.

She stroked the side of his face, smearing it with dark fluid. There was so much blood. "Clay, you're going to be OK. I'll call for an ambulance. They can sew your arm back on. You know they can do amazing things."

He shook his head slightly. "No. Too much blood." He started to choke.

She gripped his hand. "No! You're going to survive this. Clay!"

He forced a smile and she thought he had never looked so noble.

"I love you, Keri," he whispered. "I just wanted to love you."

"Clay. Clay?" He just stared at her. No, he had stopped seeing her. She buried her face in his chest and wept. "I should have loved you more."

Dr. Schelling grabbed her from behind. "We have to get out of here. More will come."

She shook him off, desperate not to leave Clay.

"No! We can't just leave him!" Then it came to her. "Wait! We can give him Lazarus9! We can bring him back to life!"

Dr. Schelling shook his head. "I don't have any here. Even if I did, he has to have it before he dies, not after." He gripped her arm. "We must leave!"

Oscar staggered to his feet. She actually glimpsed his intestines, yet his will was strong. She wondered how long it took them to regenerate new parts. He nodded toward the front door.

"We have to get to the boat," he gasped. "It's our only chance to escape." He glanced down at the mess they had made of her Clay. "It might be better this way, for him, that they never have the chance to change him."

She shook her head bitterly. "It would have been better if neither of us had met you." She leaned over and kissed Clay on the forehead. "Forgive me."

The walking wounded, the dazed dead—they left the condo through the front door and limped down the wooden deck that led to the boats. Keri carried one shotgun, Oscar the other. The men continued to bleed but their wounds were already healing. All around they heard the nervous cries of rich Orange County snobs. Yet wise folks stayed inside when shotguns were being fired. No matter, the police would come soon. There was no sign of the others but Oscar assured Keri there were more about.

Dara waited in front of the gangway that led onto the *Quintalen.* She was alone and appeared to be unmoved by their weapons, although Keri didn't know why she hadn't blown her face off already.

"None of this was necessary," Dara said calmly. "Let us put an end to it now. Come with us, we will let you all live. I give you my word."

"You murdering bitch!" Keri screamed, taking aim. Oscar stopped her.

"We're not worried about ourselves," he told Dara. "We're concerned about mankind."

"We can improve mankind," Dara said. "They need us."

"You will manipulate mankind," Dr. Schelling said. "No one needs to be controlled."

Dara studied him. "Then why did you inject yourself with Lazarus9? You say you needed to expand your research, but that was only an excuse. Your interests were more basic. You wanted to be different, superior—it's a natural desire."

"We aren't natural," Dr. Schelling said. "I see that now, why can't you?"

She spoke with unexpected feeling. Perhaps it

was feigned, Keri couldn't be sure. "Daddy, Eric is not far off. Better you deal with him than with me."

Dr. Schelling shook his head in disgust and grabbed Keri's shotgun. He cocked the weapon and pointed it at his daughter's head. "I should destroy you," he swore.

She stared, her face still stained with blood. As quickly as she showed emotion, she withdrew it. She spoke as if from a distance. "You won't. You are still too alive. You feel too much. You see something inside of me that no longer exists. Put down the gun, Daddy, give us the formula. We will leave you alone after that."

"You had me as a prisoner for a year and never got it," Dr. Schelling said. "What makes you think you'll get it now?"

Dara glanced at Keri. "The Dark One comes. That's answer enough."

"She's just stalling," Oscar complained, his shotgun leveled at her. "Get out of our way, Dara. We won't bargain with you."

Dara shrugged and stepped aside. But as they moved past her, onto the gangway, she grabbed Oscar. Not hard, almost lovingly. She leaned over and kissed him on the lips.

"It's silly but I miss you," she said. "I don't want to see you burn."

Oscar took her hands off him. "Better to burn in this world than in the next."

She nodded. "Perhaps. How is your new girlfriend?"

Keri paused and turned. "I will remember what

you did to Clay. One day I will make you remember."

Dara shook her head. "So predictable, all of you."

They boarded the boat. Dara did nothing to prevent them from casting off. In the distance they could hear police sirens. Maybe the dead in Oscar's condo were already coming back to life. Keri thought of Clay lying on the floor beside those monsters and felt sick.

The narrow channel that ran between the two jetties was deserted. Oscar feared that Dara would come after them in another boat, but for a while it appeared as if they had escaped. The sea was calm and dark; a faint breeze blew from the south. Oscar commanded the wheel, Dr. Schelling went down below to search for something. Keri stood on the bow and tried to get the image of Clay's arm out of her mind.

They were three miles out on the open water and heading north when Dr. Schelling first spotted the helicopter coming toward them.

"It must be the police," Keri said. "People must have seen us escape and told them."

Dr. Schelling shook his head. "It's not the police. Look closer, Keri, use the full power of your vision."

She did as she was told and noticed no marking on the side of the helicopter. A private party commanded the vehicle. As she strained her eyes, a side panel was thrown open and she spotted a young man who bore a resemblance to Dara lean outside the helicopter. He held a narrow hose in one hand, a high-powered rifle in the other.

"Eric," Oscar whispered, standing beside her.

"He's a hell of a shot," Dr. Schelling said. "We better take cover."

"No," Oscar said. "Remember Dara's comment about burning? Eric has a fuel hose in his hand, he is going to try to torch the boat. We have to knock the helicopter out of the sky, it's our only chance."

Sounded like a plan, but Eric was a cunning foe. He knew they had shotguns, understood that the shot would quickly disperse over even a moderate distance. The weapons were designed to take down birds, not man-made flying machines. Eric brought the helicopter almost directly above them but remained at an elevation of a thousand feet, a huge black insect waiting to strike. Oscar and Dr. Schelling each shot at the helicopter but realized they were wasting ammunition. Yet Eric carried ammunition that did not disperse with distance. Oscar took a bullet in the leg and went down. Keri knelt by his bloody side. His guts had only begun to heal and now this.

"He's going to kill us all!" she cried.

"He won't kill you and he won't kill Dr. Schelling," Oscar said as he put pressure on his wound. "But I am expendable. Jump overboard now and swim for shore. It's your best hope."

"I can't swim that far," Keri protested as she helped him with his leg.

"You can, easily," Oscar said.

"No, I'm not leaving you."

"He shot me in the leg so you wouldn't leave," Oscar said. "He could just as well have shot me in the head. Any second now he's going to . . ." Oscar stopped. The rain from heaven, the smell, was unmistakable. Gasoline, Eric was predictable as well, only it made no difference because his plans were so thorough. The fuel splashed over the deck and onto their hair and clothes.

Oscar staggered to his feet. "We have to get in the water and swim in different directions."

Dr. Schelling joined them and helped Oscar, holding his spent shotgun. He spoke with bitterness. "It looks like my son turned out smarter than his dad, after all. And that used to be my dream." He glanced upward. "He's playing with us."

A red star took birth overhead. Keri assumed the color, for her it was simply deadly fire. Yet it sparkled like a beacon, and she wondered if the police on shore would be drawn to it. Oscar grabbed her arm and pulled her toward the side of the boat.

"Jump!" he yelled. "Now!"

The star, the flare, fell slowly toward them. Keri was flying through the air, almost to the water, when it hit the deck and the boat exploded in flames. The ship's fuel tank must have detonated immediately; the shock wave hit Keri with extraordinary force and she was pounded into the surf. When she surfaced the sea was ablaze and she could not find the others. The shore looked far away but Oscar's words made sense. They could only survive by splitting up. Guilt plagued her—she

139

had got her ex-boyfriend killed and now she was deserting her new one—but she knew she should not search for her partners. Oscar was strong; wounded leg or not, he would survive.

Keri swam hard toward the distant shore lights, angling north. Many times she submerged, trying to get the hovering helicopter off her back. To her surprise she found she could hold her breath for an excess of ten minutes. After three long submarine periods, she saw the helicopter veer off and head for land. Her arms and legs were tireless, she moved faster than a dolphin. She was sure she had escaped unseen. She would make it to the shore, she told herself, find her friends, and they would get away from these monsters forever.

Because of her level of confidence, a half hour later the sight of the approaching boat broke her heart. It was not a patrol ship, and it didn't have to come close for her to spot Dara, standing casually on deck. Dara had her vision and more. Keri wondered what made her so special. Perhaps her father had shot her backside with a pint of Lazarus9. In either case, Dara was on her in minutes. She smiled and threw her a life preserver.

"We already have Ted down below," Dara said.

"Go to hell," Keri snapped. Was it true?

"That bum leg."

"You are evil."

"I am what I am, neither good nor evil." Dara leaned over the side. "All this excitement cannot be good for the baby."

Keri remained in the cold water. "I would rather drown than bring this child into the world."

Dara removed a pistol from her back belt and pointed it at Keri's head. "I'll make a deal with you. I'll kill you after he draws his first breath." She cocked the pistol. "Get in the boat, Keri. It's late and we have a long way to go tonight."

She thought of a bullet piercing her skull. Her brains splattered over the water surface. Growing new ones the same night, not sure what she would be like afterward.

Keri climbed in the boat.

11

Keri did not see Oscar until they were on shore. They were herded into a van and for a moment they were able to sit across from each other and talk. Like herself, Oscar was dripping wet, but his leg and stomach appeared healed. Dara had already fastened cuffs on their feet and hands. The material was not steel but a special alloy neither of them could break. Keri could hear cop cars in the background, but they were far away.

"They didn't get Dr. Schelling," Oscar said.

"We don't know that for sure," Keri said.

"I saw Dara's face. She's not happy."

"Where is the infamous Eric?"

Oscar glanced toward the front. He didn't seem to recognize the guy behind the wheel. "Eric won't be far," he said.

Dara opened the back of the van and climbed inside, carrying two hoods and a roll of duct tape. She sat beside Keri.

"We'll be driving for several hours," she said. "But we don't want you to know where we're going, and we don't want you to cry out." Dara held up her tools. "That's why these are necessary. But if you cooperate, I'll feed you and let you take bathroom breaks. Agreed?"

"Why do you keep me alive at all?" Oscar asked.

Dara was thoughtful. "Eric wants you dead, but that's not what I want."

"I'll never be what you want," Oscar said.

Dara tore off a strip of tape. "We're supposed to be immortal. Time will tell. It will tell us many things."

Dara shut them up and closed their eyes. Of course, had she wanted, Keri could have burst the tape. But what was there to talk about under the circumstances? She felt Dara sitting beside her as the van picked up speed and then got on the freeway. The cold young woman hardly seemed to breathe. Keri wished she could sleep, black out and cease to exist for a few hours.

They were driving for maybe five hours when Dara halted the van and took off their hoods and removed the tape. The van curtains were drawn. Dara offered them each a gallon of milk and a loaf of bread.

"I'm sorry, I forgot the butter," she said.

They were able to eat with their cuffs on. To their surprise, when they were done stuffing their faces, Dara let them use the great outdoors as a bathroom. The brilliant sun startled Keri. They were deep in the desert, on a back road that appeared to lead nowhere. The temperature was in the high nineties. Keri did not recognize the distant hills, but assumed they were in Nevada or Arizona. There were no other vehicles in the area. Dara removed their leg cuffs so that they could relieve themselves. A guy with a dark expression and a fat pistol followed Oscar off to the left of the van. Keri went to the right, Dara not far behind.

"You don't want to run," Dara warned.

"I wouldn't think of it," Keri said as she undid her pants.

Dara sighed as she strode about, restless. "Oscar's right, we didn't find Daddy."

"He could be dead," Keri said.

Dara gazed at the sky. "No. He's alive, and we'll find him."

"Running low on your precious Lazarus9?"

Dara did not look over. "The Dark One is more important than any drug."

Presently, they returned to the van and Dara reapplied their leg cuffs and hoods, leaving off the tape. There was nothing to shout about deep in the desert. Keri lay down and thought about how hard and swollen her belly was getting. She doubted it would take nine days to gestate the baby. Then what did she have to look forward to? A bullet in the brain? An incinerator? Probably Eric would forego the bullet and cook her alive.

She continued to dwell on Clay, whispered a silent prayer for his soul. She did not trust in God or eternity but she was beginning to believe in hell. What would her child do to the world? Perhaps it was cosmic justice that she should burn moments after giving birth to him. And all because she had sex with a mysterious stranger. It was a screwed-up world.

She thought of her dead sister, Debra, as well. She remembered then that she had dreamed of Debra while dying in the freezer. Her sister had tried to tell her something about the Dark One. It was odd that she was able to think of Debra now, when she had striven so hard for the last two years to blot out all memory of her. They had more in common now—they had both died.

Keri wanted to cry, to sleep, but tears and unconsciousness were denied her. She felt a hand on her leg and was stunned to realize it belonged to Dara. The witch had a soft touch; Dara squeezed her calf lightly before letting go. Keri wondered if she would ever hold her child. She almost asked Dara if she would give her a few minutes alone with the infant when it was born, but Dara would imagine she would kill it, and maybe she would. Right then, she would have killed herself if she had the chance.

"You could try to kill yourself. At this point, that might be best."

"Debra," she whispered. "Take care of Clay."

They drove for another three hours and then went underground. Keri noticed a distinct change in the air pressure and moisture content. It also got much cooler, and the sound of the van's moving echoed off nearby walls. Yet Keri was stunned at how long they drove beneath the surface, at least a half hour, although at reduced speed. She couldn't imagine such a tunnel, had never read about one.

The van titled upward, they were climbing. The humidity decreased and the air thinned. The tunnel must bore into a large mountain.

When the van halted, Dara removed their hoods and prodded them forward with a pistol. The driver got out and opened the rear doors. He also had his gun ready. He looked like one pissed-off dude, a high school lineman on steroids. Keri knew he would just as soon shoot them as look at them. They must have slowly tortured the creep to death, after his fat shot of Lazarus9.

Keri and Oscar were herded through a narrow hallway into a wide prison dug into what looked like the rear of a vast cave. Dara removed their cuffs and closed gray bars in their faces. The material was like the cuffs, an alloy they could not break. Oscar wasted no time testing it out. Dara appeared amused at his attempt.

The installation was military, Keri had no doubt. She wondered if Dara and Eric had already managed to infiltrate the government. She had doubts. She could hear almost no movement of others in the compound, too little to signal normal human involvement.

The walls of their prison were made of uneven black stone. The place looked as if it had been blasted out. They had bunk beds with fresh linen, a clothesline of naked bulbs, and what looked like a halfway decent bathroom, shower and all. Keri took several steps away from the bars and plopped down on the nearest bed. Their prison was huge, out the back way. Of course she doubted that the remainder of the tunnel led to a way out. Dara seemed to read her mind.

"There is no escape from here," she said. "Don't even think about it."

"What should we think about then?" Oscar asked.

"Where Daddy is," Dara replied.

Oscar shrugged. "I have no idea."

Dara nodded. "I believe you, I do. But Eric . . . I suspect he will want to torture you to satisfy his curiosity. I hope you don't mind."

Oscar was unimpressed. "Tell him to get on with it. There will still be no more Lazarus9. You're all going to end up like a leper colony. The truth will come out and you'll be hunted down and slaughtered."

Dara gestured to their surroundings. "But we already have important allies."

"They will not remain allies unless you provide them with the formula," Oscar said bravely, but her remark had shaken him.

"Why don't I leave you two alone, let the happy family bond?" Dara said.

"I'll need new clothes," Keri called as Dara and her crony stepped toward a thick metal door on the other side of the bars. Dara paused and glanced over her shoulder.

"I'll try to make you as comfortable as possible," she promised.

"Excluding the torture," Keri said bitterly.

Dara shook her head and a faint trace of sorrow dimmed her face. She stared at Oscar with what Keri could have sworn was longing, but then her expression iced over.

"It doesn't matter," Dara said and left.

12

Alone with her new love. Once upon a time she could have fantasized about such isolated and exotic company, but now time was the enemy. The creature in her body was her death—and already she could feel it kick.

"What should I name him?" Keri asked when they had been locked up for about one day. It was unfortunate that neither of them had a watch. Dara's goon had visited twice to feed them: bread, fruit, milk, sardines, cereal. He brought large helpings of each. Keri ate continuously and seldom had to use the bathroom. Dara had brought them several changes of army fatigues. They fit surprisingly well.

"Ted," Oscar said as he studied the walls of their prison. He was forever prowling around. He was pretty sure their cell was not bugged. He was already trying to dig his way out the back, but he said it would be another century before they saw sunshine.

"Hey, that's an idea." She paused. "What is it anyway about this *Oscar* business? Your name is Ted; why can't I call you Ted?"

He tapped on a stone and put his ear to the wall. "I like the name Oscar. Ted always sounded boring to me."

"What did your mother call you?"

"Ted." Oscar stopped and looked over. "How was she?"

"Sad. She hasn't got over your disappearance. I don't suppose any mother would." She paused. "I told her you lived in Balboa."

He sat on the bed beside her. "With the mess we left behind there, she might associate me with that condo."

"Yeah. I also told her you were an artist." Keri touched his arm. "Sorry. I should never have gone to visit her."

"It's not your fault. We just never expected that you would." He was reflective. "I would give a lot to see her again."

"Why didn't you ever go?"

"The obvious reason. When Dr. Schelling and I escaped from the others, I knew they would try to catch me visiting my parents."

"But there was another reason. You could have called and told your parents you were OK. There would have been no risk in that."

Oscar sat for a moment in silence. "They would only want to hear from their son. I am no longer their son."

"But you are, we haven't changed that much."

Oscar took her hand. "Could you go home? If Clay were alive and you had a test to take in school tomorrow, could you go there?"

Keri felt as if she had been slapped. "I don't know. I still think I'm me, but when I imagine doing what I used to do—I can't do it. You remember what Dr. Schelling said about children going insane when given Lazarus9 and dying? He believed their personalities were not formed enough to withstand the shock. I wonder if I am so different. I am only seventeen. I never had a chance to find out who I was before *I* was altered. At the same time I know none of this matters. We're locked in this prison and these jerks are going to burn us as soon as they get what they want. But I guess for my own peace of mind I wish I could die content with the life I lived."

"Were you content when you died in the freezer?"

"I was scared. But, yeah, in a strange way, I had more peace than I do now." The child in her womb kicked. "Now there is only dread."

"I wish I had died a year ago." He added quietly, "I was wrong to do what I did to you."

Her voice quivered. "Did you at least like me when you slept with me?"

"Sure. I liked you—I like you now—very much."

"But you chose me because of how I smelled?"

"Keri."

"Well, I don't understand this intuition and destiny that you were talking about."

"When I saw you I felt that I knew you."

"And that I was the mother of the Antichrist?"

"It was not that way. I was drawn to you, I saw us as inevitable."

"Because you had the Dark One whispering in your ear when you were resting?"

"Keri, stop. Eric and Dara call him that; Dr. Schelling and I never did. And I told you, he never said anything to us."

"These answers frustrate me. You and Dr. Schelling purposely set up a condition where this baby could be born, but you have no idea who he is. All you have is a vague hope that he will destroy the others."

"That is correct," Oscar admitted.

"That is stupid. If I had the guts, I would kill myself now. Kill this child." She stopped and snorted. "But that would be a panic reaction. He told me not to do that."

"The Dark One?"

"I thought you didn't call him that."

"What should we call him?" Oscar asked.

"Ted."

"Dara calls me that. How about John?"

"Why John?" Keri asked.

"That's my father's name."

She was pleased. "That's my father's name as well. John it is, we'll put it on the birth certificate.

Anyway, in my dream, John told me three times not to panic. The lines stuck in my mind because they were inappropriate. At the time I was relatively calm."

"Interesting," Oscar said. "He must have had a reason for saying it."

"Maybe he knew everything would work out all right for us."

Oscar was doubtful. "Maybe."

"Are you scared about the torture Dara spoke of?"

"I'm not looking forward to it."

"How come Eric never stops by to say hi?"

"He's probably off trying to locate Dr. Schelling."

"You really think he's alive?" Keri asked.

"Probably. Even if he had drowned, he would have come back to life."

"Do you think Eric can find Dr. Schelling?"

"The question is more can Dr. Schelling find us?" Oscar considered. "He may go to the FBI."

"Why didn't you guys do that to start with? Once you had escaped?"

"We can't let the government know about Lazarus9. It would be too tempting for them to use. But in the last twenty-four hours Dr. Schelling might have decided that he has to feed them a half-truth in order to get them to help find us. Many times Dr. Schelling and I talked about what we could tell the authorities without revealing everything."

Keri glanced about uneasily. "Are you sure we're not being bugged?"

"I can't be positive. But there is nothing we're saying that Eric and Dara will not figure out on their own."

"If the FBI does help Dr. Schelling, what are his chances of locating us?"

Oscar shrugged. "This is not a small place. It obviously belonged to the military at one time. Dara and Eric might have miscalculated taking us here. We are somewhere deep in a mountain. This facility would be hard to attack by force but is exactly the sort of place Dr. Schelling would instruct the FBI to look for."

"I don't understand their logic. Dara and Eric could have stashed us anywhere. They could have made us vanish off the face of the earth as far as the authorities were concerned."

Oscar shook his head. "They put us here because they're not sure of the power of John. Remember, it is their goal to control him, to mold him to their design."

"You think John will be able to work miracles?"

"I don't think we can imagine what John will be capable of."

"You scare me. Should I kill myself?"

"No. We can't give in to despair."

"But Debra told me to do it," Keri said.

"Who's that?"

"My dead sister. I dreamed of her when I died in the freezer."

Oscar, his face grave, did not dismiss the comment. "The only thing that makes this situation bearable is your company," he said gently.

His words meant a lot to her. But she never felt secure in his feelings for her. He had, after all, killed her once. Plus he had a secret past.

"Did you sleep with Dara?" she asked.

He looked at the floor. "Yes."

"Before or after your change?"

"After."

"How was it? I mean, you're not into necrophilia, are you?"

That made him smile. "No. I told you, Dara has a sensitive side."

"I still don't understand why she's stronger than we are. Is she stronger than Eric?"

"Yes."

"So she's the real leader here?"

"Eric pretends to lead. But I would say, when push comes to shove, Dara wields more power."

"But where did the extra power come from?"

"Dr. Schelling was never sure. Dara was different from the rest of us in only one respect—she was changed when she was near death. In fact, Dr. Schelling said that if he had waited another hour she probably would have died naturally. She was that ill."

"Why didn't he wait and inject her just before that happened?"

"He was worried about the timing. She could have slipped away before he could get the Lazarus9 into her system. Remember, you need a beating heart and flowing blood to distribute the formula."

Oscar added, "Dr. Schelling loved her very much. She was his life."

"And you guys have no real idea why some turn bad and others don't?"

"You heard our theories. They're only stabs in the dark." Oscar was reflective. "Maybe it's true that during the change demons get inside some people. There were times when I was alone with Dara that she seemed possessed. But at other times . . ." He shrugged.

"She could be loving?"

"Yes."

"Do you love her still?"

He stared at her. "Yes, and I am sorry to say that."

"Because she killed Clay?"

"Yes. And because I slept with you."

Keri forced a smile. "Oh, don't worry about me. I have a way of bouncing back from severed arms and death and demonic possession. A little heartbreak along the way means nothing to me."

Oscar gripped her hand. "I do care about you. And I meant what I said, we cannot give in to despair. Maybe we can escape." He leaned close and spoke in her ear. "You know I've started to dig at the back of the cave."

"Yes," she whispered back. "Searching for buried treasure?"

"I hear water back there. This prison is not far from an underground stream."

"So?"

"I don't know. It may be nothing. I'm going to keep digging."

"They'll see what you're up to."

"They've already seen, and they don't care. They think there's no escape."

"But I shouldn't get my hopes up?"

"No."

"Can I ask you a question?"

"Yes."

"Why can we only see in black and white?"

"I don't know. Dr. Schelling doesn't either. It is the same for everyone who undergoes the change. It might mean we're no longer fully here. That we're caught someplace between this world and the next, but that's only a theory of mine."

"It's a nice theory." She kissed the side of his face and sat back down. "Clay would have liked you if he had got to know you. You would have liked him, too, he was a nice guy and smart."

"Do you miss him?" Oscar asked.

"Yes. But I didn't miss him enough when he was alive. Now my feelings don't count. They don't do him any good."

"That's not true. Death might be the end, but your sister spoke to you. Maybe she and Clay are waiting for you, on the other side. He might be here right now, and finally know how you feel about him."

Keri put a hand to her face. For a detached corpse, her grief was a hard bump on the road, as palatable as the stone walls that imprisoned them. Even so, she could not push it away. The pain seemed to flow to her from the other side, out of time and reason, from a netherworld where her child waited to emerge. Despite what Oscar told her, she wondered if she should kill herself, before it was too late.

"I wish I could believe that," she said quietly.

13

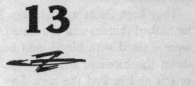

Keri's belly continued to grow as Oscar kept digging. Different members of the goon squad brought them food and time passed. Keri rested but was still unable to sleep. The baby seldom stopped kicking; he would not require sleep either. Oscar was kind to her but they didn't kiss again. Keri was never free of the feeling that Dara was watching them. Keri suspected that even Eric didn't know all of Dara's plans.

On what could have been the fourth day, when Keri was about seven months pregnant—give or take a few hours—Dara came for Oscar with a gun. Her younger brother wanted to question him, she said. Keri admired Oscar's courage; he nodded and gave Keri a thumbs-up as Dara led him away. Keri's heart broke right then. She must have loved him because she wanted to share his pain. But she knew her rival would stand beside him when Eric started the torture. Dara might even hold Oscar's hand and whisper sweet things in his ear, she was that kind of girl.

They kept Oscar a whole day. When he returned he looked thinner and exhausted. His army fatigues were stained with blood, and he was forced to lie down the moment the goon shoved him into the prison and locked the bars. She took his mangled hand, kissed it lightly, and stroked his face. He was having trouble breathing, and she suspected they had cracked his ribs.

"What can I do?" she asked.

He closed his eyes. "I'll be all right in a little bit."

"Was Eric there? Did he do this to you?"

"Yeah. That guy, he wouldn't have missed it for the world."

"Did you tell them anything?" Keri asked.

"No way. Just my name, rank, and serial number."

She carefully laid her head on his wounded chest.

"We are doomed," she muttered.

Two days later Keri started to get contractions. Dara happened to be on hand, delivering food and flirting with Oscar, and quickly sprang into action. Three goons appeared and wheeled an elaborate hospital bed into the prison. It was equipped with stirrups, an IV, and a bright overhead lamp—the whole nine yards. Keri had not given much thought as to who was going to deliver her baby, but right then an understaffed and underpaid HMO would have looked good. Again, Dara seemed to read her mind.

"Don't worry," Dara said as she helped Keri onto the table. "Eric has hired the finest medical help. The doctor will be here in minutes."

"I don't want Eric here," Oscar snapped.

Dara touched his face. "The protective father, cute. I'm sorry to say this is one show Eric is not going to miss."

"Oh God," Keri mumbled as she lay back on the bed. Eric would make a home video of the delivery and post it on the Internet. See the birth of the antichrist! Only five dollars at *revelations.com!* Ask about our literature! We've got a product that can make you look younger forever!

A slight young guy with curly blond hair appeared. She didn't need a formal introduction; he had Dara's features, and, besides, she already glimpsed him when he had leaned out of the helicopter and squirted them with gasoline. Eric was dressed entirely in black; the revolver in his belt was probably silver. He didn't look scary at first glance, another skinny punk kid with attitude. But his eyes were a horror. When Keri looked into them she saw a vacuum. The demon that had entered him during his change had been from a cold hell. Eric showed no reaction upon seeing her. He gestured to a nearby goon, who carried an Uzi. Keri felt her water break, a simple phrase for what felt like a disgusting mess.

"Bring in Dr. Wolen," he said flatly. Eric ordered

her pants removed. Keri felt so violated—no one thought to avert their heads, not at first. But then Dara asked the goons to leave and Keri felt grateful despite herself.

The doctor arrived a few minutes later and Keri was relieved to see that at least he looked the part: elderly, gentle bedside manner, thick glasses, intelligent face. He wore a white coat and carried a large black bag. He had brought instruments and drugs. After a brief examination of her pelvis, he asked if she wanted something for the pain. He offered her Demerol through the IV or an epidural to block sensation in her lower body.

"No drugs," Eric interrupted.

The doctor looked at him as if he were a spoiled kid. "I'm in charge here. I don't care how much money you're paying me."

Dara intervened. "This is a special patient, Dr. Wolen. We explained that she is a criminal, but we did not tell you about her unusual physiology. She is stronger than she appears. She will have this baby faster than normal."

Dr. Wolen shook his head. "She has scarcely begun to dilate. The baby will be some time."

"Listen," Eric said to the doctor. "We are paying you thirty thousand dollars for this delivery. When we tell you something we mean it. This girl is to have no drugs. We do not know what effect they will have on the baby."

Dr. Wolen was losing patience. "They will have almost no effect on the baby. I am the expert here,

I have been doing this for forty years. I would prefer it if the bunch of you left the room."

Again Dara intervened. "We have told you about the security issues here. We cannot leave the room. Deliver the baby as professionally as you can, and we will pay you your money and you can go."

Dr. Wolen shook his head. "I did not agree to these conditions."

"It doesn't matter," Dara said firmly. "These are the conditions and you will have to abide by them."

Keri feared that the doctor would get angry and leave. But he sighed and turned his attention back to the job at hand. With each contraction Keri felt pain, but her transformed body took it well. Her insides were supernaturally strong, and she felt she had incredible control over her abdomen and pelvic muscles. She merely had to will herself to dilate and she could feel the baby moving. Dr. Wolen examined her again and shook his head in wonder.

"I have never seen this before," he muttered.

"Keep breathing," Oscar said as he held her hand and tried not to look at Eric and Dara. But the brother-sister team was omnipresent. Keri tried not to think about what her child's birth meant for her. Occasionally giving her an encouraging word, Dara did not seem to be in a mood to put a bullet in her brain. Yet this was the same girl who had ripped off Clay's arm. Dara had no loyalty except to herself.

Keri grimaced up at Oscar as a powerful contraction shook her.

"How do you feel about becoming a daddy?" she gasped.

"Excited." He added, "Wish the circumstances were different."

"Don't we both," Keri agreed.

The baby came too quick—Keri's control was not as absolute as she thought. She tore badly and felt herself bleeding. Dr. Wolen worked to stem the tide. Somewhere out of sight she heard her son cry. Dara confirmed that it was a boy, but Keri could not see her child. It seemed Eric had snapped him up. Keri felt a wave of desperation even as the pain of her injuries began to decrease. Her tear was already beginning to heal. Dr. Wolen continued to mutter to himself.

"This is not possible," he said.

Dara turned to her brother and helped wipe off the baby. Oscar tried to have a look at him but Eric drew his gun and motioned him away. Dr. Wolen had seen enough, he straightened indignantly.

"This is inappropriate," he said. "I don't care what this young couple has done. They cannot be treated this way at a time like this."

Eric smiled thinly and handed the child to Dara. He approached the doctor, sliding his gun back into his belt. "In your opinion, Dr. Wolen," he said, "is the child healthy?"

Dr. Wolen glanced toward Dara and her crying bundle. Keri continued to struggle to see her son but was denied the opportunity.

"I have not had a chance to examine him, but he appears fine," Dr. Wolen said.

"Fine. Then we can reward you for your services and you can go."

Dr. Wolen shook his head. "I have to attend to the mother." He turned back to Keri. Eric grabbed his arm.

"That is not necessary," Eric said.

Dr. Wolen glanced at his arm and back at Eric. His puzzlement deepened; no doubt Eric had a tight grip on him. "Let go of my arm," Dr. Wolen said, a note of fear in his voice.

"Please," Eric insisted, bringing his crazed expression within an inch of the man. Keri could not bear to see what was to happen next but watched anyway. She figured the show was over for all of them. It was tragic, so much digging at the rear of the cave and Oscar had never reached his underground stream.

She wanted so much to see her baby!

"Don't panic," she whispered to herself, in vain.

"Don't play with him," Dara said as she cooed with the crying baby. If nothing else he had a healthy set of lungs. Eric giggled and released the doctor's arm.

"I'm so sorry, Dr. Wolen," Eric apologized. "How much did we say we would pay you?"

The doctor sensed danger. "Thirty thousand, in cash."

Eric slapped his leg. "That much? What if I told you we lied?"

"What do you mean?" Dr. Wolen mumbled, taking a step back.

Eric stepped forward and grabbed him by his white coat. "I mean, what if we only brought you here to make sure the baby was delivered safely and that now we intend to murder you? What would you say to that, Dr. Wolen?"

Dr. Wolen paled and glanced down at the hand on his coat.

"Please let me go," he pleaded.

"Eric," Dara said impatiently. "Stop."

Eric glanced at Dara and let go of Dr. Wolen. He shrugged helplessly.

"What can I do?" he asked. "I have to stop."

Dr. Wolen swallowed. "I will take my fee now and leave, if you don't mind."

Eric lost his smile and stared at him. "I don't mind. Except there is no fee. Except I do intend to kill you."

Dr. Wolen shook his head slightly. He finally saw that the young punk with the bad attitude was actually a sadist. He tried to back up but bumped into Keri's table.

"N-no," Dr. Wolen stammered. "I have a family. I will just leave. You don't owe me anything."

Eric smiled, brief, a fraction of a second. "We owe you, Doctor. And you owe me, for not listening when I spoke." He studied the doctor. "How do you want to die?"

Dr. Wolen shook his head and continued to back into the table.

"You cannot be serious," he gasped.

Eric came to a decision. "I will rip out your liver. How does that sound?"

Like a cornered animal, Dr. Wolen appealed to Oscar. "Help me!"

"I'll take care of this," Dara said angrily, handing the baby to Oscar. In quick strides she crossed the floor and punched the doctor square in the face. Blood splattered around her palm, spitting dark drops on the floor. The blow brought a sickening sound of broken bone and cartilage. Dr. Wolen stood for a moment and then toppled to the floor, dead before he knew what had hit him. Dara turned to Eric and scolded. "This is a special moment and you've ruined it. You purposely annoy me. Why?"

Eric shook his head. "Who gives a damn?" He nodded to the baby, who had begun to settle in Oscar's arms. "What do we feed him?"

"Mother's milk would be the logical answer," Dara said, wiping her bloody hand on her pants and turning to Keri. "But I have a deal with her. She has to go."

Eric snickered. "Are you jealous?"

Dara cast him a hard eye. "Are you foolish?"

Eric did not back down. "She has to live at least until the baby doesn't need her anymore." He pulled out his gun and pointed it at Oscar. "But I never saw the need for the father."

Oscar was nonplussed. "Funny. I never saw the need for assholes like you."

Eric grinned and cocked his gun. "You do have spirit."

Dara firmly pulled down her brother's weapon.

"Let us leave them alone with their child, for now," Dara suggested. "They are no danger to us."

Eric glanced at the baby. "I don't like this arrangement."

"And no one likes you," Dara said. She grabbed Eric's arm and pulled him out. But she glanced back before she disappeared through the metal door. "Take care of him, Keri. You know he's our future."

Keri finally received her son—Oscar laid him gently on her chest. His hair was dark and fine, and he looked so much like his dad that her heart swelled with love. For Keri, despite the insanity of the setting, he could not have been more beautiful. Yet his eyes were very dark; he seemed to watch her with an awareness of secret things.

Dr. Wolen continued to lie on the floor. No Lazarus9 for him, Keri thought, the poor man. Oscar could give him a decent burial in the rear of the cave. She worried about the man's family, as she worried for the whole world. Yet a wave of unlooked-for hope swept over her. Her son, John, stared up at her as if he knew her and her thoughts.

"The future is not set," Keri said to herself.

14

John grew. Keri ate and fed him. Oscar dug. John grew so fast Keri had to eat every thirty minutes to keep her milk flowing and John happy. But after two days, when he was biologically two years old, he took his own food. He could talk by then but seldom chose to do so. When he was five days old, ready for kindergarten, all he did was read off the Internet on the computer he had requested Dara install. Dara did not argue with him; no one felt so inclined. The connection was one way; they were not allowed to send e-mail to ask someone to rescue them. To say John was not a normal child would have been like saying Jesus had other talents besides carpentry. John read at ten thousand words a minute with perfect recall and devoured an entire set of encyclopedias in one afternoon.

But whose god were they living with?

Keri asked herself the question constantly.

John was a strapping ten days old—in fifth grade going by stature but possessing the equivalent of twenty Ph.Ds in knowledge—when he tired of the Internet and told Dara to bring him seeds and fertilizers. She asked why and he merely stared at her.

"I want seeds and fertilizer," he repeated.

"What kind of seeds?" Dara asked from the other side of the bars.

"Mainly vegetable seeds," John replied, in a solemn tone, sitting on the corner of one of their beds. He never needed to rest. He was a serious child. He had not smiled since he had stopped breast feeding. He looked more like Oscar each day, although his eyes and hair were darker. John added, "But you can bring me a few tree seeds as well: oak, birch, cedar, and olive."

"Those things will not grow down here," Dara warned.

"They will," John said. "Bring extra water, too."

Dara was curious. "Wouldn't you prefer to come with me, outside, and plant your seeds there?"

"No," John said.

"Why not?"

"I will remain here."

"Are you finished with the computer?" Dara asked.

"Yes. You may take it away."

"But maybe you will want it later?"

"No," John said.

"Have you learned all you need to know on the Internet?"

"I have learned all it can teach me."

"What will growing vegetables teach you?"

"You would not understand."

"Try me," Dara insisted.

"No," John replied.

Dara went to fetch the seeds and fertilizer. She was the demon squad's only liaison with their child prodigy. Eric had withdrawn into the unseen background. Perhaps he still searched for his father. Keri honestly could not say she missed Eric's company. Oscar had buried Dr. Wolen at the rear of the cave after a short prayer ceremony. Oscar still believed in God; Keri was afraid to believe in her son.

Keri called John over after Dara left. He would obey her if she insisted, but she did not push when it came to discipline. One thing he disliked was clothes. It was all she could do to keep shorts on him. He came and sat beside her on her bunk bed. An experiment had occurred to her. She handed John a large pad of paper and a pencil.

"I want you to do me a favor," she said. "I want you to draw your father and me a picture of how you see yourself."

He stared at her quizzically, an alien expression on him. He normally possessed such assuredness in his gaze that she worried that soon they would appear like well-trained apes to him.

"I do not see myself," he replied. "I am myself."

"Do you remember where you were before you were born?"

"Yes."

"Where were you?"

"You would not understand."

"I need you to help me understand. That is why you need to draw us a picture of how you see yourself."

"That is not possible."

"Why not?"

"I am myself."

"Very well, going back to where you were before you came here, can you draw a picture or image of how we—here on Earth—would understand you in such a place?"

"Yes."

"Will you draw a picture of that right now for your mom?"

"Yes."

"Thank you, John. You know I love you very much."

He began to draw. "I know."

Oscar wandered over and studied his son. "Interesting idea, Keri."

"Thank you. How's the digging going?"

"The underground stream gets louder each day."

"When you reach it, do we drown?"

"Probably," Oscar said.

"You heard of John's request for seeds and fertilizer?"

"Yes. I wouldn't mind fresh produce."

"How can he get it to grow down here? These bulbs . . . there is no sunlight."

"It will be fun to see how he does it," Oscar said.

John was an extraordinary artist. Keri had never seen him draw before but was not surprised at his talent. She suspected he was an excellent musician as well. When he had asked for seeds and fertilizer and refused to explain why, Dara had obeyed him and would until she knew better who he was. John showed them a certain allegiance or else he would have already left the prison. His loyalty to them must concern Dara. Keri hesitated to count on it. The truth be known, she still feared her son. John was only ten days old but had no real equal or master. Where did human love fit in the complex equation of his life? He had never told her he loved her, although she said the magic words to him several times a day.

John finished his drawing and handed it first to his father. Oscar stood and stared at it a long time before sighing and closing his eyes. Oscar was always pale but now it was as if his blood had turned to tap water. He handed the sketch to Keri and she understood the reason for his shock. A knife plunged deep into her heart. Truly, they must have committed great sin in the past to deserve the present. A scream erupted deep in her throat but fell to a strangled sob as it passed her lips.

"Do not panic," John said.

Cloven hoofs, a barbed tail, horns.

John's picture of himself.

The devil.

15

Keri tore up John's picture and tried in vain to rest. She lay on her bed and strained to convince herself that John was playing with her. The only problem was that John had not a trace of a sense of humor. John drew what he drew because it was accurate. For the father of all lies, he was remarkably straightforward.

Which brought her back to the central issue. Should she attempt to kill her son? Maybe he could make plants bloom deep beneath the earth—that remained to be seen—but he showed no signs of being physically stronger than they were. They assumed he could protect himself if he had to, but Keri had her doubts. If she sneaked up on him from behind, grabbed his head and broke his neck, she didn't see how he could stop her. Of course her physical ability to kill him had no link to her emotional ability. Merely thinking of the idea made her sick to her stomach. And Oscar wouldn't do it, he loved his son as much as she did.

What to do?

Do not panic.

Why did he say that?

Dara brought seeds and fertilizer, and John planted a garden with more care and love than he had ever shown toward any of them. He spoke to the ground and the seeds as he worked. Actually, John was in the habit of whispering to things none of them could see. They had assumed he was merely talking to himself, but it was something else Keri wondered about. Maybe John was really an extraterrestrial from a planet named Hell. The saucers would soon come and cart them off to eternal damnation. Her mind was all over the place, it was almost impossible to love someone whom she feared so deeply. But love him she did, and so she let him grow.

John's garden bloomed in six days, just in time for his sixteenth birthday. He was a handsome young man, with long dark curly hair and eyes as black as the space between galaxies. He still disliked clothes, but she managed to keep cutoff army fatigues around his waist. For his birthday they had fresh corn on the cob with peas and carrots. Dessert was oranges—John had grown them as well. Dara joined them for the meal, and it was clear she did not know what to make of their budding antichrist. Keri had not shown Dara John's picture of himself.

"Why do you like to grow things?" Dara asked

John as they ate. John had developed the habit of sitting cross-legged on the ground when he was not working on his garden. He looked up from his plate when Dara spoke.

"You would not understand," he said.

Dara set her food aside. "I tire of that response, John. I want you to help me understand."

John stared. "Your understanding would be limited. It would only confuse, and you would feel more tired."

"Try me," Dara insisted.

John glanced at Keri, who nodded for him to try. Dara noted that John had turned to her, and the brief exchange seemed to fill Dara with doubt. But she hid it quickly and leaned forward to listen to John's explanation. John also set aside his plate of food.

"This you consider non life," he said, pointing to the ground, before gesturing to his garden. "This you consider life. You see a distinction between the two. But there is no distinction. One comes from the other. The other will return to the one." He picked his plate back up and continued eating. "That is the way it is."

Dara frowned. "I don't understand. Explain more."

"No," John replied.

Dara turned to Oscar. "Do you understand?"

"Gimme a break," Oscar said. "Whatever philosophy he's teaching, it's way above my head."

"I don't think he's trying to teach at all," Keri interrupted. "He only responded because he was

176

pressured to do so. I doubt John is here to enlighten humanity."

"Then why is he here?" Dara asked, a note of frustration in her voice.

Oscar chuckled. "Certainly not to help you with your childish plan of world domination. Look at him—you think you can control him? He doesn't care what you do."

Dara spoke softly. "Maybe he would care if he was threatened. Or something he cared about was put in danger."

"You could try torturing us in front of him," Oscar suggested.

"Or you could attach electrodes to his brain and shock him into obedience," Keri added. "God, Dara, you never learn. Your bad-girl persona gets boring. You're afraid to kill us because it might anger John, and you're afraid John is not going to help you rule the world. For a kick-ass bitch, you show no guts."

Dara stood. "You're risking a lot talking to me this way."

"When you've got nothing, you've got nothing to lose," Oscar said, quoting Bob Dylan. "You have nothing to threaten us with. Sit down and finish your vegetables. John is going to cook us zucchini and cauliflower tomorrow. If you behave yourself maybe he will invite you back."

To their surprise Dara sat down and picked up her plate. She appeared conflicted. "I hate this place," she muttered.

"Can we go to Hawaii?" Keri asked hopefully.

"Maui is nice this time of year," Oscar added.

Dara looked at him. "Why do you keep digging?"

"For the exercise," Oscar said.

"There is nowhere for you to go," Dara said.

Oscar munched on a carrot. "What are you asking?"

"Why you don't join us?"

Oscar shrugged. "You're the bad guys. I'm one of the good guys. Besides, I'm kind of attached to Keri and John here. And they're never going to join you."

"No one knows what John's going to do," Dara remarked.

"True," Keri said. "But Eric is predictable. Sadists usually are. How can you align yourself with him and hope to get to where you want to go?"

Dara gestured. "He's my brother."

"He *was* your brother," Oscar corrected.

Dara gave him a hard look. "Did you ever tell your wife the things we did together immediately after your change? Or did you choose to present her with the PG version of your past achievements?"

Oscar was unmoved. "I did what I did to fake you out. And it worked—sucker."

Dara sneered. "You faked all that pleasure I gave you?"

"It wasn't that great," Oscar muttered.

Dara threw down her plate and stood and glared down at Oscar. "You two will die here, in this hole, you know that! What is wrong with you, Ted?"

178

"He prefers to be called Oscar," Keri muttered. Looked like the Dragon Queen had finally caught fire—showing emotion and all, such bad taste in a detached zombie. Keri could see the sources of her frustration but still did not pretend to understand Dara's mind. The young woman was unpredictable. Oscar kept eating and acted nonchalant.

"I guess I just got bored with you," he said.

Dara threw her head back and laughed. "And so you want to die with this drab girl?"

"Die? Been there, done that," Oscar said. "Remember?"

Dara quieted and pointed a sharp finger. "I could take off your head this second."

"Yeah, yeah, I know how strong you are," Oscar said. "Why don't you go take a couple of aspirin and lie down and rest?"

Dara went to snap back but was interrupted.

From his place on the floor, eating his lunch, John spoke.

"Yes, leave," John said. "Now."

Dara had never heard him give an order before. None of them had. There was power in his voice. Dara turned and left them alone.

She did not return for lunch the next day.

THE GRAVE

16

The day of reckoning finally arrived, six days later. John had stopped growing by then, at a glorious twenty days. His dark hair was down to his waist and he was built like a god. All he cared about was his garden, though, it had expanded to fill most of their prison area. They had apples and plums and bananas three times a day. John merely had to talk to his trees and they gave him fruit.

But the good guys had come to kill the bad guys, finally—they heard shooting and shouts beyond the metal door and figured Dr. Schelling and the government had located Dara and Eric's secret hideaway. Oscar was excited by the development, but Keri cringed.

"They will kill us before Dr. Schelling can rescue us," Keri said.

"They might try to do that," Oscar said. "But we're not easy to kill."

They heard explosions, screams of pain, gunshots getting closer.

"Dr. Schelling brought heavy artillery," Oscar observed.

"It doesn't sound like his help is taking any prisoners," Keri said. "What do you think he told them?"

"That this gang is infected with a genetic mutation that is worse than the plague," Oscar said. "It was one of the ideas Dr. Schelling and I talked about."

Keri nodded. "But we are infected, too, as far as the boys in blue know."

"They might think that way," Oscar admitted. "Dr. Schelling was obsessed to blot out any trace of Lazarus9."

"Yet he wanted John as much as the others," Keri said.

"John might be our ace in the hole," Oscar agreed. No pun intended—their prison hole suddenly seemed a vulnerable place to be. Yet John was not interested in the fighting beyond the door. He was planting celery and string beans and talking to invisible spirits. Keri had to call out to get his attention.

"Honey," she said. "We will have visitors soon. We don't know if Dara and Eric will get to us before they do, but we might need your help." She paused. "Can you help us?" She had never asked him such a question before.

"What do you want?" he asked.

"We would like to escape from here alive," Oscar explained. "With you. Can you help us?"

John did not blink. "We will see what happens."

Keri sighed. "I feel I am about to panic."

Oscar pointed to the rear of the cave. "I told you yesterday I think we only have to punch through that last boulder to get to the underground stream. That might be a way out."

"You also told me that the stream would probably flood this place if you removed the boulder," Keri said.

"It's a backup plan," Oscar said.

"Tell me our main plan?" Keri said.

"John is right, we will have to see what happens," Oscar said.

A lot happened and very quickly. Darling Dara and Evil Eric suddenly burst through the metal door and shot off the lock on their prison bars. Both were armed to the hilt with automatic weapons and spare ammunition. Both were bloody; they had taken a few hits but no doubt had given worse in return. Eric in particular looked a mess. He had taken a gruesome blow to the right knee—cartilage and bone showed but he had lost none of his energy and enthusiasm for being a jerk. Pointing a machine gun at them, he ordered them up against the wall. His mood was foul.

"How did they find us?" he demanded of Oscar.

"I suspect your father told them to search for a megalomaniac's dream castle," Oscar replied.

182

"Maybe we shouldn't piss him off right now," Keri whispered.

Dara secured the metal door and came close. "There are a lot of them. Daddy must have given them plenty of details. They are using some type of thermo explosives that incinerate everything in their path."

"Have you tried to surrender?" Keri asked.

"Let's just say they aren't interested in discussing terms," Dara replied.

Eric was furious. He waved a gun at John.

"You have to stop them! They will burn you as well!"

John glanced at his garden. It was the only thing he was worried about. He did not reply to Eric's outburst, which did nothing to soothe the bad boy's nerves. Eric put his gun to the side of Oscar's head.

"Our father will be spearheading this attack," Eric said. "You have to talk to him, reason with him."

"What possible reason could I give him for letting you survive?" Oscar asked.

Dara forced Eric to lower his weapon.

"We are all in this together," Dara said. "I also believe Daddy is in charge of the operation. He has fried three-quarters of the rooms in this facility. The people under him are not checking to see who is around the next corner before they set off their explosives." She glanced at John. "I think he has had a change of heart about our mutual experiment."

"Maybe that is not such a bad thing," Oscar remarked.

"Shut up!" Eric snapped.

"Are all your people here?" Keri asked.

"Don't tell her anything!" Eric shouted.

"What difference does it make now?" Dara yelled at him. Then to Keri, "Yes. We kept them here so that we could keep an eye on them."

"Hard to find good help these days," Oscar said.

Dara shrugged. "They are probably all burned by now."

Eric paced restlessly, limping. "I am not going to burn."

Dara was exasperated. "Then we must form a plan quick." She looked at John. "Do you have any ideas?"

"Do not panic," John said.

Dara shook her head. "Swell."

The metal door exploded open three minutes later. The sound was deafening, the shock wave a flat fist—Keri was knocked off her feet. Smoke and fumes poured over the sparking rubble. They expected a massive charge, but a single figure in an isolation suit walked in. He carried a large square package of explosives in his hands. Even through the fogged suit visor they could see his beard. Oscar helped Keri back up.

"I am alone," Dr. Schelling said. "Put down your weapons."

"Like we'd listen to you!" Eric sneered.

Dara studied the package her father was carrying.

She eased her gun straps off her shoulders. "Eric," she said calmly. "Do what he says."

"No!" Eric swore. "I'll shoot the bastard first."

Dr. Schelling held up a blinking detonation switch. "Shoot. It doesn't matter. It ends here, for all of us. This plague must stop."

"What did you tell the others?" Oscar asked.

"Does it matter?" Dr. Schelling said. "They know that everyone in here must be destroyed."

"You planned this from the start," Keri said. "You just wanted to create your Dark One so that you could gather the others."

Dr. Schelling pulled off his head gear and sighed. "That was not my intention when Oscar and I escaped. But after witnessing the brutality of the attack at the condo, I saw no hope for any of us, on either side." He studied John. "Who are you, son?"

"It does not matter," John said.

Dr. Schelling fingered the detonator. "My life's work has become a nightmare."

"Do not panic," John said.

Dr. Schelling sweat as he fingered the detonator. "What do you want from us?"

"What do you want?" John asked.

"Daddy," Dara said gently. "Help us escape. Eric is a pain in the ass and I have misbehaved, but we are still your children. We can forget all about Lazarus9 and go live in Hawaii." Dara acted wounded. "I don't want it to end this way any more than you do."

Dr. Schelling had tears on his face, not merely sweat, and Keri had thought him incapable. It was as if the brilliant scientist loathed every cell in his body. But his children were a part of his body—he did not want to let go of them, and he knew he had to.

"You're poison," he groaned as his fingers stroked the bad-news button on the fat bomb in his shaking arms. "We're a disease that must be stamped out."

They heard sounds from the tunnel behind the ruined door.

Soldiers on their way. Orders to kill.

Had Dr. Schelling told them he intended to commit suicide?

"This is bull!" Eric snarled as he lifted his gun and aimed.

"Don't!" Dara shouted. But supergirl was too slow this time to make a difference. Eric shot his father in the leg and the scientist fell to his knee. Seeing an opportunity, Eric limped forward with his weapon blazing. Dr. Schelling's face turned to a bloody mass but he was still conscious and he still had his finger on the detonator. Dara chased after Eric and tried to tackle him, but she was conflicted about her plan. Her hesitation cost her a step while Eric continued to shoot up their dad. Oscar grabbed John and Keri by the arms.

"It doesn't matter who pushes the button, this place is going to burn!" he shouted. "The underground stream is our only way out!"

Keri had to agree. The three of them raced to the rear of the cave. Oscar and Keri gripped the huge rock that barred their way. Keri could hear the fast current through the stone walls. But even with their superhuman strength, they could not budge the boulder.

"You should have loosened it more!" Keri complained.

"I planned to do so today!" Oscar shouted back.

Behind them they heard more soldiers. Eric swore and Dr. Schelling shouted out—the guy was still alive and kicking. Dara cried out as well but the point was already well taken. The government operation was entering its last stage. Fry them all, this place is a den of evil. Keri and Oscar turned to their son with anxious eyes.

"John," Keri said. "Can you move this rock for your mom and dad?"

John glanced back in the direction of his garden.

"OK," he said.

John stepped forward and tugged on the rock.

Their world exploded in cold black water.

Keri felt herself being lifted up and slammed against a wall. The blow almost knocked her unconscious. She did not know if she had been swept from the prison or rammed deeper into it. Out of the corner of her eye a brilliant ball of flame blossomed. The torrent was momentarily pierced with exploding bubbles and violent vapor. But as quick as it took form, it was snuffed out and Keri was racing through a wet tomb. True, she could hold her breath a long time since the change. She was not a fish, however; she needed to breathe sometime, and as far as she could tell from the pounding her body was taking on the rock walls around her, they were not rushing toward a bright exit. She wished she could find Oscar's hand, see her son one last time.

Frantic minutes passed. The pain in her chest grew and there was no way to alleviate it. The water was ice—she could almost have been back in the grocery store freezer, slowly dying without understanding. Yet there was a difference this time. The pain was greater, but at least now she saw a pattern that had led up to her end. Destiny had chosen her for this role because she had wanted to be different from everyone else. Fate moved with irony—the universe had granted her wish and made her so different that now it felt obligated to bury her in the bowels of the earth to cover up the mistake.

But what could she have done differently?

Her lungs breathed fire. Keri had to open her mouth.

The water put out the flames. The pain stopped.

Keri died. Everything was forgotten.

All was silent. Blessed silence.

Epilogue

A garden. A place for souls to go at the end of life. Paradise filled with warmth and light. Enchanted nature stretched for endless miles.

It was like her dream in the hospital.

She lay on sandy ground beside a vast lake, trees and hills climbing up behind her. The water was cold and still, a mirror of loveliness. She was half naked, but it did not matter because the sun was hot. She didn't remember opening her eyes but they were open now. A black-and-white postcard surrounded her, an unspoiled national park. She was alive—the underground stream had led somewhere, after all, dumped them drowned in the lake. No problem for those taking Lazarus9.

She sat up and saw Oscar and John standing beside the lake. Oscar was teaching John how to skip stones. There were still a few things their son did not know how to do.

"Hey," Keri called. "Are we in heaven?"

Oscar looked over and smiled. "I was wondering when you would finally heal. We've been up for hours."

Keri carefully climbed to her feet. "Where are we?" Except for the three of them there was not a soul around. Oscar came over and patted her on the back. John knelt and studied a plant at his feet.

"I think we're in Arizona, but I'm not sure," he said. "It doesn't really matter. We can walk out of this place."

"Sounds good to me. But I hope we can get a lift from someone along the way. I'm starving." She called to John. "Honey?"

John looked over but did not come.

Oscar took her hand and spoke quietly. "He's not coming with us."

"What?" She felt a lump in her throat. "He has to come. We're his parents."

"We talked while you were unconscious. He says he has to remain in a natural environment, away from people."

"Why?"

"He didn't explain." Oscar stared at their son with affection. John pulled a leaf from the plant he was studying and tasted it. Oscar added, "But I have an idea why."

"What?" Keri said.

"I think we have misunderstood him from the beginning. Whatever he was going to do, we were sure he would change the world. And perhaps he will do that. But I think he came to change the world in a way that has nothing to do with humanity."

"I don't understand."

"He has told us many times that we can't understand him. But I have been thinking about that picture he drew of himself and the way he can make plants grow. Also, I have studied the way he seems to communicate with unseen beings." Oscar paused. "Do you know where the word *panic* comes from?"

"No."

"It is from the Middle Ages. It is derived from the word *Pan.* Do you know who Pan was?"

She had to think. "Isn't he the king of the fairies?"

"He was the king of all the elementals: the fairies, the gnomes, the dwarves, and the elves. According to legend, Pan has cloven hoofs, horns, and a barbed tail. In the Middle Ages certain people supposedly saw him and associated him with the devil. That is why his name is linked to the word *panic.* His coming—to those who did not understand him—used to inspire fear. Maybe each time he told us not to panic, he was telling us not to give into the misunderstanding that surrounded his true nature."

"That's a ridiculous idea. You're saying John is the incarnation of Pan?"

"It's just a theory. I thought you said you liked my theories."

"Have you asked him if he is Pan?" Keri said.

"Yes. He didn't say no. He told me I couldn't understand. But I don't think he is the devil. Look at him, he loves every type of plant and tree. I think what he was trying to tell us in the cave is that he is a link between the earth and living things. No, I say that poorly. I think he sees the earth as a living being, filled with elementals that are anxious to build forests and gardens everywhere. Maybe that's how you were able to give birth to him. Pregnant with my seed, you were stuck between the living and the nonliving.''

Keri felt relieved. "So he's not the antichrist? He's a gardener?"

Oscar smiled. "I think he's the greatest gardener who ever lived. Alone out here, given years, God knows what he will accomplish. Humanity has polluted every corner of the globe. Maybe John will be able to fix the damage. That is, if we leave him to do his job." Oscar added, "We have to let him go, Keri. He's bigger than both of us."

She felt pain but knew Oscar spoke the truth.

She walked over to say goodbye to her son.

"John," she said. "We're leaving now. May I say goodbye?"

He stood up from his plant and waited.

She kissed him on the cheek. He did not respond.

"You take care of yourself?" she said.

"Yes." He stared. "Mother?"

"Yes, John?"

He smiled faintly. "I will remember you."

She hugged him hard. "You better," she said.

They did not find a road until they had walked to the other side of the lake. It must have been off season—they hiked all day without meeting a single camper.

The asphalt road wound out of the forest and down the mountain. But near dusk they spotted a ranger's sport utility vehicle coming from behind them and flagged it down. The vehicle slowed and pulled over to the side of the road.

Dara Schelling sat behind the wheel.

"Can I give you guys a ride?" she asked.

"Christ," Keri moaned.

"How did you make it out of there?" Oscar asked.

Dara shrugged. "I have a few tricks up my sleeve. But don't worry, Eric and Daddy didn't survive."

"You're sure?" Oscar asked.

"Quite sure."

"Are you crushed?" Keri asked.

"I get over things fast." Dara paused. "Where's John?"

"Off saving the environment," Oscar said.

Dara was not surprised. "He was never much interested in people."

"Where's the ranger?" Keri asked.

"He's in the trunk," Dara said.

"Sport utility vehicles don't have trunks," Keri said.

Dara put a hand to her mouth. "A pity. Then I don't know where he is." She leaned out the window and patted Oscar's hand and spoke sweetly. "So you want a ride?"

He withdrew his hand. "I think I'll pass."

Dara glanced at Keri. "Because of her? I won't hurt her, you know, not today."

"Let's just say I don't think we're compatible anymore," Oscar replied.

"Suit yourself." Dara put the vehicle in gear. "It's a long walk to civilization."

"Don't worry, we'll be fine," Keri said.

Dara ignored her and blew Oscar a kiss. "Later."

"Later," Oscar replied.

Dara drove off down the mountain.

They continued their hike. It would soon be dark.

"You're not going to see her again, are you?" Keri asked.

"No."

"You're sure?"

"Yes." Oscar stopped and pulled a roll of mints from his pocket. "Would you like a peppermint?"

"Sure." She took one. "Will we always have this metallic taste in our mouths?"

"I don't know, I suppose."

"Why peppermints? You got me to buy them as well."

"Dara turned me on to them."

She grumbled. "That bitch."

"Don't be jealous."

"You would be in my situation."

"There's no need." He shocked her. "Do you want to have another kid?"

Keri blushed. "We're supposed to be dead. Can we?"

"I have no idea. We can try."

She liked the sound of that. She took his hand.

"Let's try real hard," she said.

About the Author

CHRISTOPHER PIKE was born in Brooklyn, New York, but grew up in Los Angeles, where he lives to this day. Prior to becoming a writer, he worked in a factory, painted houses, and programmed computers. His hobbies include astronomy, meditating, running, playing with his nieces and nephews, and making sure his books are prominently displayed in local bookstores. He is the author of *Last Act, Spellbound, Gimme a Kiss, Remember Me, Scavenger Hunt, Final Friends* 1, 2, and 3, *Fall into Darkness, See You Later, Witch, Die Softly, Bury Me Deep, Whisper of Death, Chain Letter 2: The Ancient Evil, Master of Murder, Monster, Road to Nowhere, The Eternal Enemy, The Immortal, The Wicked Heart, The Midnight Club, The Last Vampire, The Last Vampire 2: Black Blood, The Last Vampire 3: Red Dice, Remember Me 2: The Return, Remember Me 3: The Last Story, The Lost Mind, The Visitor, The Last Vampire 4: Phantom, The Last Vampire 5: Evil Thirst, the Last Vampire 6: Creatures of Forever, Execution of Innocence, Tales of Terror #1, The Star Group, The Hollow Skull, Tales of Terror #2, Magic Fire,* and *The Grave,* all available from Archway Paperbacks. *Slumber Party, Weekend, Chain Letter,* and *Sati*—an adult novel about a very unusual lady—are also by Mr. Pike.

CHRISTOPHER PIKE'S

The Last Vampire

THE ANCIENT MONSTER.
THE MODERN HERO.

Collector's Edition, Vol. 1

INCLUDES

THE LAST VAMPIRE
THE LAST VAMPIRE 2: BLACK BLOOD
THE LAST VAMPIRE 3: RED DICE

Collector's Edition, Vol. 2

INCLUDES

THE LAST VAMPIRE 4: PHANTOM
THE LAST VAMPIRE 5: EVIL THIRST
THE LAST VAMPIRE 6: CREATURES OF FOREVER

From Archway Paperbacks
Published by Pocket Books

POCKET
BOOKS

1472-02

Christopher Pike